BROWN SKIN, WHITE LIES

THE LIES WE TELL TO BELONG

BOBBY MOHAN

WHAT READERS ARE SAYING

Brown Skin, White Lies: The Lies We Tell to Belong by Bobby Mohan is a hauntingly bittersweet story of an international student's struggle in Australia.

Brown Skin, White Lies is a gripping, slow-burn novel that follows Arjun Ajith Nair, a debt-ridden student from Kerala, navigating the harsh realities of international life in Melbourne. As Arjun juggles cultural shocks, exploitative jobs, and escalating threats from a predatory loan shark, his journey spirals into survival, reinvention, and quiet resistance. What begins as a personal struggle unfolds into a harrowing account of migrant exploitation, culminating in shocking twists and a haunting moral reckoning. Boldly written with emotional depth and sharp prose, this is a unique, character-driven story that rewards readers with a powerful, unforgettable ride.

From: **Miguel Da Costa** <draft-autosave@protonmail.com>

To: **Rekha Gurung -** and to anyone digging through abandoned inboxes

18 Nov · 02:17 a.m. - **Ras el-Ain, South Lebanon**

Rekha,

If the "From" line jolts you, good.

Miguel Da Costa is the alias that buys me a mattress above a falafel shop.

Arjun Ajith Nair is the name you once hurled across tram platforms and mango rows- the name I still answer to when no one's listening.

Everything that followed- Melbourne side-hustles, Kununurra sap-burns, Broome nights that never quite end sprang from a single evening in Pampady, Kerala.

We called it *beef-fry night*: pepper-black, chilli-red. *Achan* and I mapped an Australian MBA onto a greasy plate, sure that spice could season luck.

Morning disagreed. Bank token C-17 blinked REJECTED,

scholarships vanished like steam, and the pharmacy deed trembled in *Achan's* pocket.

Enter Roy Joseph, trailed by a cloud of Old Spice and a serpent grin. His bridge loan gleamed like mercy: tuition covered, interest later, signatures now. We toasted with Bru Gold, though it tasted of pennies on the swallow.

Then came the airport. *Amma's* A\$ 2 jar of garlic pickle rattled in my carry-on. One wrong tick-box, one A\$ 90 "inspection fee," and the jar spilled more than brine. That white lie nudged the first domino; the rest toppled fast:

- courier shifts in Melbourne alleys
- predator hunts no résumé should list
- heat-warped secrets drifting beneath Kimberley stars
- a Border-Force notice stamped CONDITION 8202–DETAIN/REFER

The full splash pattern- debts, detours, whatever might still float- took me months to stitch. It sits in the attached *Brown Skin White Lies.doc*. Read it at your own pace; may it earn- not forgiveness, perhaps-but a little understanding.

Every alias and every kilometre loops back to that table: beef fry cooling, debt reheating, luck changing temperature with each breath.

Until the ledger balances or the battery dies, expect more drafts like this. Follow the splashes if you dare.

- Miguel (for now)

Brown Skin, White Lies.doc

―――――

You're about to open a file.
Just notes — loosely in order, with a few flourishes where memory got bored.

Some parts ramble. Some read like forms.
But it's all true — or true enough to carry weight.

Read slow. Judge light. Stay to the end.
This is how I survived. And survival rarely edits for style.

FILE ONE
വീട് · VEEDU
HOME

Pampady: the leaking house where pepper beef and bank forms birthed the loan that won't die.

1 BEEF FRY NIGHT

Pampady, Thursday, 6 October 2016

7:15 p.m.

Pampady evenings start in the wok: an iron pan black as temple soot, buffalo meat spitting under a hail of pepper, chilli and curry leaves. Exhaust from the bus stand drifts in, mixes with cumin, settles on your lungs like down-payment smoke.

Biju's Makeshift Mess has six plastic tables and exactly zero cutlery. You eat beef fry the way God and the GST office intended - right hand, first three fingers, no witnesses. The place suits us: cheap, dim, judgment-proof.

Achan sits opposite me, khadi shirt still smelling of antiseptic from the pharmacy. He worries the callus on his thumb, last week's sugar-test prick that refuses to heal. When I ask if it hurts, he shrugs. "Only when results come out."

We are not here for dinner; we are here to talk about **forty lakh rupees** (*Seventy thousand Australian dollars, if you round up and hold your breath*) without the town listening. Beef in Kottayam buys you that privacy: the respectable folk won't step inside after dark.

Achan pinches a cube of meat, dips it in gravy, lifts it to his mouth. The beef oil stains his cuff in the shape of a comma; the sentence after that comma is his:

"Tomorrow, after opening prayer, we see the loans officer. Bring your mark sheets, the MBA brochure. Printed-serious."

He says it lightly, but the tumbler of watered-down gravy trembles on the metal table. Inside my head a slide-show flicks: Melbourne skyline, tuition line, the imagined red stamp-**APPROVED**-that will let us breathe. I burn my tongue on chilli and hope.

Two auto drivers at the next table argue about the cost of petrol and visas.

·   ·   ·

"My cousin blew ten lakh, came back cleaning toilets in Dubai."

"Still toilets with air-conditioning, da."

They laugh. I count the zeros of ten lakh on my greasy palm.

The clank of bracelets announces **Roy Joseph**- safari suit, cologne that could disinfect a ward. He ducks inside, scans the room, spots us.

"Ajith-*ettan*, Arjun-*mone*!" He doesn't sit; he looms like unseasonal rain.

"Tomorrow is the bank, no? Take two copies of the property deed," he advises, voice loud enough for the frying pan.

Achan smiles, half-bow. "Bank first, Roy-*etta*. Cheaper interest."

Roy laughs, taps my shoulder- a friendly hammer. "If they blink, call me. Bridge loan ready. No boy should miss February intake."

He leaves a business card face-up on the table- **Laxmi Financials: Fast Cash, Friendly Terms**- then strolls out, white Maruti already idling. Biju's neon splashes ambulance light across the bonnet.

. . .

Achan exhales. "Helpful man," he says, but his tone tastes of antacid.

Biju arrives with a rag, winks.

"Flying soon, Arjun-alle?"

"In-shallah," I answer; in Pampady, every language shares the same *maybe*.

I pay ninety-rupee notes, still smelling of Dettol, from the cash drawer at the shop. Outside, KSEB street-lamps flicker; a power-loom coughs its shift to a halt. Pepper heat clings to our shirts, or maybe it's dread; both sting the same.

Halfway home, *Achan* breaks the silence:

"If it's God's plan, the loan will pass."

"I studied probability, *Acha*. God's plan charges interest."

He almost smiles, presses the pharmacy keys into my fist, camphor, rust, resignation.

. . .

Amma waits at the compound gate, sari tucked, hair unbound. She reads our faces, opens the door wide enough for tomorrow to squeeze through.

I lie on the coir cot, ceiling stains mapping last monsoon's leaks. A rooster misreads the hour and crows too early or too late, same thing. On the stool, the clear folder glows under a bare bulb: mark sheets flat, brochure front, no folds, no stains. I whisper the tuition figure once, then the loans officer's name like an opposing mantra.

Sleep comes in small loans-repayable at dawn, accruing by noon-and somewhere, behind Biju's kitchen, an iron pan cools but never forgets the flavour of debts discussed over beef.

2 TOKEN C-17

State Bank of Travancore raised its shutters at 9:02 a.m., a two-minute delay that felt like interest accruing in real time. Inside, ceiling fans only pushed the humidity around; Lakshmi's portrait above the counter stared down through a garland bleached the colour of stale turmeric.

Achan and I pulled **token C-17** from the red dispenser. The LED board glowed at **C-11**-six approvals between us and whatever the gods of collateral had decided overnight.

In my lap: a clear folder. Mark sheets pressed flat. Melbourne brochure on top, tuition circled- **₹ 40 lakhs**. My palm fogged the plastic; wiping only smeared the worry wider.

. . .

At the opposite row, two young staffers unwrapped idlis from a newspaper and popped them straight into their mouths- no cutlery, no shame. I envied the ease.

C-12, C-13...

C-14

A goat farmer in cracked sandals emerged grinning, sanction letter fluttering like monsoon relief.

C-15

Jeweller's daughter-approved.

C-16

Tyre-shop owner- approved with guarantor.

Hope rose, cruel and sharp.

Just then, through the glass door, **Roy's white Maruti** idled at the curb, AC running.

He spotted us, lifted two fingers in a lazy salute, and mouthed *"Call me."* Then the car eased away toward Bazaar Road, exhaust curling like a signature.

· · ·

The display pinged.

C-17

We stepped through the half-door into the cool sanctum of clerical power. The loans officer, round spectacles, saree pleated into geometric obedience, didn't invite us to sit.

"Applicant: Arjun Ajith Nair- son of Ajith Nair?"

Achan nodded once; I found a dry *"Yes, ma'am."*

She read the file, front to back, then again, eyebrows twitching like typewriter hammers. Finally, she reached for the red stamp, aligned it with surgical care, and pressed:

REJECTED

The ink shone wet, arterial.

"Insufficient collateral," she recited, voice the temperature of distilled water. "For overseas programmes, we need liquid security of at least sixty per cent." Two firm taps on the brochure total. "Your pharmacy valuation covers forty-two."

. . .

Achan's mouth opened, closed. I counted ceiling-fan blades-three-and the crack that ran between them-five-anything but the stamp.

She slid the folder back. "Reapply with added security or consider private financiers." She nudged a pastel flyer forward- **Laxmi Financials • Fast Loans • Friendly Service**- and turned to beckon **C-18**.

———

Outside, noon heat bounced off the granite steps and slapped us. *Achan* adjusted his khadi shirt pocket; the pen inside suddenly looked ornamental.

Neither of us spoke down **Bazaar Road**. Sunglass peddlers, honking tempos, the constant arithmetic of onions per kilo-fifty-six rupees today, even tears cost a premium. At a tea stall, we stopped; two rickshaw drivers argued petrol hikes while sluicing hot chai from glass tumblers into their palms, bare-handed and unburned. I tried to copy the gesture, scalded my fingers, said nothing.

Achan's first words came out like a diagnosis. "We still have Roy."

He didn't add *cheaper*; the bank's stamp had already priced that illusion.

· · ·

Across the road, the Maruti was back, AC humming. Roy stepped out, safari suit crisp as balance-sheet paper, and waved us over with the ease of an auctioneer who knows the reserve has just been met.

The folder in my hand felt heavier than any textbook. It wasn't paperwork anymore; it was collateral looking for a buyer.

The Maruti door clicked open, cash register, mousetrap, same sound. *Achan* squared his shoulders first. I followed, heat hammering inside my skull.

Somewhere behind the temple wall, a noon bell rang-one, two, three-counting rupees we did not yet owe, but soon would.

The meter started the moment we sat down.

3 BRIDGE MONEY

The office squats above a pawn shop whose flaking façade still promises **CASH FOR GOLD**. One rusted staircase, two flickering bulbs, and a single room: two desks, one wheezing fan, and the ammoniac tang of over-worked toner. Behind the bigger desk, a nine-inch statue of Velankanni Mary, blue mantle chipped, LED halo twitching, stands guard beside a "Customer First" poster bleached to social-studies grey. Her plastic sorrow gazes straight through the ledger where Roy Joseph enters new souls, compound interest already whispering the Hail Marys.

Roy rises as we enter, safari suit crisp, smile already itemised.

"*Chettan*, Arjun-sit, sit. Tea?"

Achan declines. I couldn't swallow steam, let alone tea.

. . .

Roy opens a green ledger, clicks a navy-blue ball-point like a starter's pistol.

"Bank said no?"

Achan nods once.

"Not a tragedy," Roy purrs, uncapping the pen as though it were a scalpel. "We bridge."

The Numbers (read aloud like scripture)

- **Total MBA spend:** ₹ 40 lakh.
- **Bridge today:** ₹ 6 lakh cash, right now.
- **Use-case:** Confirmation of Enrollment deposit, visa fee, first-semester insurance, airfare. "Show the Aussies you're solvent," he winks.
- **After visa:** State Bank will happily reopen, release semester tranches. "Banks love risk- once it's offshore."
- **Interest on bridge: 3 % flat per month** - ₹ 18,000 every 30 days (≈ A$ 360).
- **Security:** half-cent paddy deed, a blank cheque, and his eyes flick to my collar- the gold chain *Amma* pressed into my palm last Onam.

Two pages of eight-point type. One shiny revenue stamp. Roy slides the agreement across.

· · ·

Achan signs first, thumb trembling on the ink pad. I sign next; my name looks foreign beside so many zeroes. Roy whistles, stamps his own flourish, tears off our copy, counts nine warm bundles of thousand-rupee notes. Each rubber-band snap lands like a pistol shot.

He holds up his Nokia torch-phone; the tiny screen glows:

FIRST INSTALMENT: 10 May 2017

"Clock starts when immigration stamps your passport," he says, voice as soft as temple sandalwood. He pockets our blank cheque, then adds, still smiling-

"Lose my number, Arjun, and I'll dial your mother instead."

———

Sunlight outside is a hammer. *Achan* tucks the envelope deep inside his khadi shirt as though heat might melt the currency. A jeweller's shop bell rings below- another gold chain surrendered to someone else's dream.

My phone vibrates before we clear the curb: **Roy** again.

Mone, you can fly wherever you want - but remember, debt has a home address. And your parents still live there.

Clock running already.

————

I repack the folder: loan agreement on top, bank rejection buried, brochure last, like a prayer card, no temple accepts. Then a fresh sheet:

₹ 40 lakh goal

– ₹ 6 lakh bridge (3 %/mo)

– hopeful ₹ 20 lakh bank loan (10 %/yr)

– ₹ 4 lakh family gold

Balance to earn → ₹ 10 lakh

→ A$ 18,000

→ 200 burger shifts

Simple maths.

2 a.m. A lone mosquito taps the net; the ceiling-fan blades chop soupy air. Each rotation sounds like one rupee of interest. By sunrise, the room will owe Roy another twenty-five.

Sleep arrives in fragments, collateralised by dawn.

. . .

The idol downstairs keeps smiling; the clock upstairs keeps billing.

4 MOTHER'S PAWN RECEIPT

Pampady, Tuesday, 11 October 2016

Amma claimed she needed turmeric.

That was the pretext for walking me past the junction, past the tea-stall gossips, past the grocery that actually sells turmeric- straight to **Subramanian Chettiar Jewellers & Pawn**. The shutters were half-down for midday prayer, but the old man knew a pledge when he smelled one; he cranked the grill up the rest of the way and waved us in.

Inside, the air tasted of varnish and fear. Fluorescent tubes hummed over glass counters lined with bangles that would never meet the people who forged them. A single wall fan laboured above the scales.

. . .

Amma loosened the cloth knot at the top of her handbag and slid two gold bangles onto the felt: plain ninety-six-gram designs, wedding-gift weight, daily-wear memories. Chettiar flicked on his loupe, twisted each piece like he was wringing out sentiment, then placed them on the brass scale. The needle steadied at a number that could finance two weeks of tuition, or three months of interest payments to Roy.

"Twenty-two karat, nothing fancy," he said, voice mechanical, as if he were pricing tapioca.

Amma nodded once. Her eyes never left the bangles, but her shoulders had already surrendered.

Chettiar counted out cash in thousand-rupee notes, fanning them to show their faces. He wrote a receipt in looping Malayalam, tore it, and slid it across.

PLEDGE VALUE: ₹ 72,400

REDEMPTION WITHIN 120 DAYS - INTEREST 1.9 % PER MONTH

Amma's thumbprint bloomed on the carbon copy like a blood-orange bruise. My signature trembled beside it, co-pledger, guarantor, son.

Outside, the sun seared the asphalt. *Amma* tucked the cash

into a cotton purse and knotted it twice. Only then did she speak:

"Don't tell *Achan* until fees are paid. One worry at a time."

I nodded, throat pulp-dry.

On the way home, we passed the grocery that actually sells turmeric. *Amma* bought a ten-rupee packet, because lies, like receipts, need timestamped camouflage.

Back at the house, she slid the pawn stub under the coffee-tin rice jar, the place she keeps spare keys and small secrets. The bangles' absence left two pale bracelets on her wrists, ghost circles catching the afternoon light.

That night, while *Achan* balanced the pharmacy ledger, *Amma* grated coconut for dinner one-handed, the other hand resting on the empty skin of memory, as if the bangles were still there and she could feel their weight.

I lay awake counting interest:

₹ 72,400 × 1.9 % = ₹ 1,376

per month, *46 rupees* every sunrise-

a metronome louder than the ceiling fan.

Some debts accrue on paper; others circle your mother's wrists, invisible but furious.

5 THE TEMPERATURE THRESHOLD

Kottayam, Monday, 10 November 2016

The air-conditioner inside **Kottayam Diagnostics** exhaled clove-chilled fog while November sun hammered the roof. My phone buzzed in my shirt pocket:

Roy: "₹ 18,000 due by midnight, no grace. – RJ"

The message stung hotter than the fever creeping up my neck.

At reception, I signed the TB-X-ray register, ballpoint snagged as if it too doubted my lungs. Above us, a red LED ticker bled warnings: **TEMP > 37.5 °C → RESCHEDULE / EXTRA FEE ₹ 650**. Every heartbeat sounded like a coin dropped in Roy's counting jar.

. . .

A nurse in strawberry-pink scrubs slid a glass thermometer beneath my tongue.

"Too much chai?" she asked.

"Too little sleep," I mumbled around the stem, vowels misting the glass.

Thirty breaths. I prayed to Vishnu, to the Reserve Bank, to whichever god accepted decimal bribes. **Beep.** She read, frowned, tapped, read again.

"Thirty-seven point four. Borderline. Sit ten minutes, drink water. One more try. Cross thirty-seven-five and you pay again next week."

A reschedule meant two extra days of Roy-rate compounding. I swallowed a full jug, hoping dilution counted as medicine, and dabbed my forehead with the pawn-receipt gone soggy in my palm.

Second reading: **37.3 °C**- a mercy degree. She stamped **FIT FOR X-RAY**, tore a strip of paracetamol (₹ 48) from a blister pack, and I paid with notes still fragrant of Dettol.

I stepped outside, pocket buzzing with borrowed time, tongue coated in chalk and the faint aftertaste of surrender.

I blinked at the sun, dizzy with relief and dehydration, the kind that makes you feel like God's just granted you a second chance—but only until lunch.

5:40 p.m. - A-to-Z Medical & General

Neighbour-uncle with gingivitis breath hovered over the cough syrup shelf.

"So, *mone*, bank loan flopped, alle? Heard Roy Jacob floated you- very high interest!"

He laughed, slapped the vaccine bruise on my shoulder.

"Education costs everywhere, Uncle," I said, barcode gun trembling around a box of vitamin D. Inside, **37. 3** felt like **39**.

———

7 10 p.m. - *Vishu* Procession Office

The *chenda*-committee secretary met me at the gate, mundu starched, blade-sharp.

"Eda, we struck your name off. Boys who stay in Pampady will drum."

. . .

He pressed a consolation coconut-laddu into my fever-dry palm. Inside, the drums began practice without me- sticks cracking rhythms my ribs already knew. Each beat stamped one word: **REPLACED**.

———

9: 05 p.m. - Kalluvila House

Amma laid **seven plates, though only five guests came- coconut rice, chemmeen fry, pineapple pachadi,** the farewell spread. Halfway through, Aunt Lakshmi unclasped two thin bangles and slid them toward *Amma*.

"For buffer, chechi. Melbourne isn't a ration shop."

Achan's jaw set. "Enough has been pawned. We won't beg at our own table."

He slid the bangles back; they chimed against a steel tumbler, tiny cymbals of stung pride. Aunt blinked fast but kept silent. I bit a prawn shell by mistake; salt-blood met chilli on my tongue.

The LED bulb buzzed like a mosquito trapped in glass. Fever or shame- both burned the same wattage.

• • •

Phone on the windowsill vibrated again-Roy's reminder ringtone, no text this time, just vibration measuring every delayed rupee. *Achan* raised a glass of warm water.

"To safe journeys," he said, voice steadier than his hand. We echoed. Aunt's bangles lay forgotten beside the pickle jar-two rings of muted gold, calculating what pride costs per gram.

I slid a paracetamol past my shredded tongue; it lodged like a coin in a payphone. The thermometer in my pocket pressed my thigh, a silent auditor.

Interest Clock: T-0 h - Balance ₹ 18,000 (due tonight)

Sleep issued in micro-loans-repayable at dawn, compounding by noon-while somewhere behind our house a cooking fire died. The night cooled, but the debt kept its fever.

And as the house dimmed, I realised: no god accepts late payments.

6 EXPORT DREAMS, IMPORT LIQUOR

Pampady, Tuesday, 20 December 2016

Pampady's lone liquor licence hides in a low-roofed bunker behind the bus stand. By day, it doles out watered toddy in plastic sachets; after dusk, the shutters lift, the sign sprouts fangs - **BLUE MOON BAR & FAMILY RESTO (A/C)** - and the town's men file in to drown whatever can't be pawned.

Tonight, the bar hums like a transformer about to blow. Ceiling fans whip rum fumes and fry oil into a single, flammable cloud. Bollywood hits from seven summers ago throb out of a speaker balanced on a crate of empty Kingfisher bottles. A neon crescent over the till blinks - every third blink fails, like hope with a stutter.

. . .

The floor tiles sweat under spilled soda and ghosted debts, sticky enough to trap sandals and small regrets.

Roy has annexed the only "VIP booth": Formica table, two cracked plastic armchairs, one bench steeped in Old Monk. His grin is wider than the bar's licence.

"*Achan*, Arjun! Sit - export dreams deserve import liquor."

A waiter in a wilted Santa hat takes the order: three large pegs of McDowell's No. 1, soda separate, beef-fry double plate. Bells jingle in the pom-pom as he vanishes.

Achan lowers himself like a man accepting anaesthetic. I perch on the bench, knees grazing sticky vinyl. When the tube light flares, Roy's gold ring throws spears of light across the table.

The drinks land. Roy pours with a surgeon's steadiness, setting our tumblers so close their rims kiss.

"Before we toast, one small housekeeping."

He opens a slim black notebook - names in neat biro, a final blank line labelled **Default Fee**. Tap.

· · ·

"Three per cent flat on six lakh."

Tap.

"Eighteen thousand on the tenth."

Tap.

"Delay costs two per cent a day - motivational interest."

Each tap is gentle; the message lands like a gavel. *Achan* nods, knuckles whitening around his tumbler.

The notebook closes with a whisper of paper- no louder than a scalpel returning to its tray. Roy raises his glass.

"First toast: to hard currency and harder schedules. Cheers."

Rum scorches down. Roy drains his glass, replaces it precisely where it stood - no spill, no shift.

He slides a manila envelope across.

"Forex slip - twelve thousand Aussie dollars. Upload tonight; algorithms watch timestamps."

I file it into my backpack; his thumb lingers on the fold a beat too long.

. . .

Roy's phone vibrates. He checks but does not answer, letting us read the screen: **Caller: Varkey (Collections)**. The smile never leaves his jaw, but the torch in his eyes clicks off.

"People think interest is numbers," he murmurs. "It's a clock with teeth: wind it, it grinds; forget it, it bites."

Achan manages a brittle laugh. Round two arrives; Roy pours again.

The third peg loosens *Achan's* consonants. Roy's voice softens - velvet on steel.

"*Chettan*, nobody here wants trouble. Pay on time - no calls, no visits. Life stays tidy."

A pause, weightless yet loaded.

"The opposite is... untidy."

A siren wails past the junction; Roy tilts his head, timing the fade.

Then he drains the glass and clamps *Achan's* shoulder - friendly, except the fingers settle on the collarbone like a mechanic testing worn brake pads.

"Sleep well. Interest never does."

. . .

Neon paints Roy blue as he dissolves into the lot. Our auto idles beyond the gravel; the driver half-dozes over the meter. *Achan* shivers, though the night is warm. I steady him into the back seat.

As we rattle through dark streets patrolled by stray dogs, my phone buzzes:

Roy: Interest doesn't sleep, da. And neither should you.

I don't reply. Just stare at the screen and wonder if Roy ever needed alarm clocks - or if he lets the debtors do the waking for him.

Ahead, the pharmacy sign glows faint green; behind it, an unseen meter ticks ₹ 25...₹ 50...₹ 75... for every hundred seconds the tyres turn.

I pay the driver ₹ 140 - tipless- and guide *Achan* inside. *Amma's* sari rustles in the dark corridor; she doesn't switch on the light.

Rum and interest linger on my tongue in equal measure. I slide the remittance slip beneath my pillow, feel the pledged chain's cold weight on my chest, and close my eyes to a clock that doesn't need hands to keep perfect time.

7 PACKING THEOLOGY

The dining room has become a departure lounge with no boarding gate.

Cardboard cartons, half-zipped Samsonite, torn rupee envelopes: every surface a mini-altar to logistics.

Amma presides like a priestess of weight limits, sari pleats pinned back, hair twisted into a knot that means business.

First, she lays out the **essentials of exile** on the floor tiles-each item announced like a chant:

1. **Garlic pickle** in a recycled Nescafé jar, oil sealed beneath two layers of cling wrap.

"For homesick rice," she says.

2. **Chilli powder** (extra-hot Byadgi) double-bagged, tied with red thread.

"Melbourne wind bites; this bites back."

3. **Curry-leaf packets**, sun-dried and brittle, tucked into the toes of my sneakers "so Customs dogs won't sniff history."

4. A fistful of **vibhuti coins**, one pressed into every pair of rolled socks, warding cold feet, of any variety.

The smells-tamarind, roasted fenugreek, chilli throat-sting-rise like incense, sanctifying twenty-nine kilos of ambition.

————

Achan counts cash on the table-what's left after fees, forex card loading, and Roy's first interest set aside.

The notes look thin, spread in labelled piles: **OSHC, taxi to Cochin, rent bridge-week**.

He wordlessly slides ₹ **2,000** into my diary margin-"buffer for anything," scribbled in his neat English.

Outside, neighbourhood aunties conduct a last-minute audit through the grille gate:

• **Chandran-*mama*** lobs in cones of plantain chips.

• **Rekha-*chechi*** presses a travel-size jar of Vicks into my palm-"Melbourne winds forget their manners," she winks.

• Someone's cousin recycles warnings: "Dollar crashed three rupees yesterday- watch your semester drown."

. . .

Laughter circles the courtyard, but keeps glancing at the calculator in *Achan's* hand.

Amma pours rose-milk into steel tumblers; condensed-milk sweetness coats every good-luck toast.

I taste sugar, but behind it hovers the metallic tang of interest.

———

10:12 p.m.

Suitcase weigh-in: **29.7 kg** (allowance 30).

Jeans lose to textbooks; textbooks lose to a pickle jar wrapped in three socks.

10:45 p.m.

Mark-sheet folder slid into outer pocket.

11:03 p.m.

Gold chain (pledged but not redeemed) taped inside undershirt; receipt taped inside diary.

Midnight.

A lone auto-rickshaw coughs into the lane, meter bulb blinking like a nervous heart.

Amma seals the Nescafé jar inside a plastic grocery bag, double-knots it, then slides it between the shirts.

If homesickness has a colour, it's the oil floating on this pickle.

That amber-orange slick, clinging to the lid, refusing to mix.

Here, under foreign light, it shimmered like a memory half-translated.

Maybe that's what homesickness is - not grief, not nostalgia - just this oily presence that refuses to disappear, floating on top of everything. Too pungent to ignore. Too familiar to throw out.

"If Customs asks, say it's medication," she jokes, but her eyes read worry:

A\$ 413 fine for undeclared food- the price of nostalgia, payable at Tullamarine.

Achan snaps the suitcase shut- zipper's final rasp sounds like a verdict.

She hands me a small plastic pouch of **chilli powder** to keep in hand luggage "in case the checked jar bursts."

The powder is the exact shade of sunset we're leaving behind.

· · ·

At the threshold of packing dramas and futures not yet lived, I stand before what is to come - and what will soon become memory. Something thick and red and unnameable slides down my throat and doesn't leave.

It tastes like garlic, debt, and goodbye.

8 TEMPLE TO TULLAMARINE

Pampady, Tuesday, 14 February 2017

Dew webbed the jackfruit leaves, incense curled from neighbour courtyards, and Pampady blinked awake- milk packets thunk, temple bells cleared their throats.

We stopped at the soot-black *fly-over Ganapati-* the cramped alcove where petitions skip the middle managers of heaven.

Amma circled camphor three times, pressed a coconut into my palm.

"Break it clean."

One strike, shell split, water arced- transaction logged. The priest rang the bell once: receipt stamped.

Back on the road, the shattered shell rattled on the kerb, like destiny's castanets.

———

At **9:30 a.m.,** the Tempo Traveller nosed into our lane-
twelve bodies, fifteen opinions, one Samsonite at bursting
point. There was no packing left to do- only ceremonial
redundancies:

• plantain-chip cones for nostalgia,

• voltage adapter "because Aussie plugs glare like angry
eyebrows,"

• exchange-rate horror stories disguised as jokes.

Rain began past Ettumanoor, drumming the roof like
overdue interest. *Achan* audited folders- passport, IELTS,
COE- then audited them again; enumeration the last thing
he still commanded.

Amma slipped her plastic *Guruvayoor* key-ring into my fist.

"Keep your pockets loud with blessings."

———

Cochin International: Terminal glass gleamed bureaucratic
gold. Check-in scale blinked **29.8 kg**-proof *Amma* had
smuggled two jars of garlic pickle inside a Head & Shoulders
bottle without cracking the 30-kilo ceiling.. The clerk tagged
the bag like a minor verdict.

. . .

Security wand chirped at the key ring; guard waved me on. Immigration rifled blank pages for future sins, then stamped **DEPARTED**-half blessing, half eviction.

Behind the barrier, family arranged themselves into a silent constellation: *Achan's* shaky V-sign, *Amma's* jasmine-wilted palm on the glass. Their breath fogged and failed to cross.

Phone buzzed:

Roy: "When you land, da- Australian address. Clock starts when wheels kiss runway."

No "safe flight," just an audit trail waiting for an update.

———

Kuala Lumpur International Airport shimmered like prosperity on hire-purchase. Durian ghosts clung to recycled air. Selvan- the floor supervisor whose shoes whispered harsher truths-offered a packet of **murukku**.

"Homesickness fits in carry-on," he said, half rueful.

At the transit desk, a Malay-Indian couple fretted that Customs might confiscate their dried chillies. Home hadn't snapped; it had stretched.

· · ·

Roaming fees glared; Roy's ringtone stayed silent. Relief and dread arrived together- twins who never speak.

————

Cabin lights dimmed. Snore- chorus in six dialects. Arrival card asked *Intended length of stay*; pen hovered, *four years? Until staplers stop biting?* I wrote **Temporary**. Permanence attracts duty.

5:40 a.m. -fluorescent sunrise, reheated omelette. Suburbs unreeled below, neat and treacherous as exam grids awaiting my first wrong answer. Tyres kissed Tullamarine asphalt; a collective gasp rippled the fuselage. Kerala's comma became a full stop; Melbourne opened with a capital debt.

Phone hunted signal- I silenced it. Alarms could wait until baggage reclaim; one last unmetered breath before Roy's ledger resumed its tally.

Welcome to Arrivals. Roy's interest made it before I did.

FILE TWO
கடம் · KADAM
DEBT

*Melbourne: fines, SIM cards, and Roy's stopwatch turning
every swipe into compound interest.*

9 ARRIVAL-HALL ALGEBRA

Tullamarine, Wednesday, 15 Feb 2017

6.45 a.m.

They hand you Australia on a mustard-yellow card - tick-boxes for soil, seeds, or contagious optimism.

I lied with the precision of a tuition-fee spreadsheet: **NO** to "food items," even though *Amma's* garlic pickle and two kilos of chilli powder were vacuum-sealed in my backpack like contraband planets.

One lie felt like a rounding error on ₹1.5 lakh of airfare begged from three lenders.

Immigration officer raised one eyebrow to half-mast.

THUNK. Visa stamped. Conscience downgraded.

"Welcome, mate."

Mate scraped my tongue like an unseasoned *dosa* pan - but I was through.

———

Baggage carousel five spun futures in polycarbonate.

A beagle sniffed beside a bio-security officer, nose twitching like a customs oracle.

It froze beside a Japanese tourist's duffel.

"Declared food, sir? No?"

"That'll be a four-hundred-and-thirteen-dollar mistake."

Everyone patted pockets for imaginary fruit.

My pulse performed full Bollywood choreography.

Pickle suddenly sounded like chemical warfare.

Carousel slowed, groaned, stopped.

No black Aristocrat. No fluorescent FRAGILE tag.

Nothing.

Lost luggage: karmic surcharge for lying.

———

At Baggage Services, a woman in a hi-vis asked for a contact.

"Still getting an Australian SIM."

"Hotel?"

"Share-house."

"Address?"

"Twenty-three Cactus Court, Thomastown." Spelled it twice.

She typed like the keyboard owed her rent, then handed me a claim receipt - the bureaucratic equivalent of *thoughts and prayers*.

————

Airport Wi-Fi came with an ad tax: three bars, one lifeline.

Amma: Ate something, *mon*?

Achan: Did Roy call?

Me: Reached safely. Will message after SIM. Love.

No mention of the missing bag - or the bio-fine that might follow it.

Sliding doors parted. February wind slapped, carrying winter's résumé in a summer font.

A PA crackled:

"Passengers from Kuala Lumpur flight AK214, baggage may be subject to Quarantine inspection upon delivery."

. . .

My stomach sheared sideways.

When that suitcase finally reached Cactus Court, a customs van might follow - invoice in hand, lie spelled with my name.

———

Outside waited a city I'd sold to my parents as certainty.

Behind me: a carousel that owed me fabric, pickle, and proof I existed.

Empty-handed, half-invented, I stepped onto Australian concrete and prayed my future would arrive before the chilli did.

10 POST-IT PARLIAMENT

Thomastown, Wednesday, 15 Feb 2017

The SkyBus brooded outside Terminal 2, a red brick daring gravity to move it.

One backpack, a lost-baggage receipt, and the echo of a P.A. warning about "quarantine inspection" were all I carried on.

Driver in navy turban raised an eyebrow.

"Light packer, eh?"

"Minimalist by accident," I said. Panic, it turns out, travels carry-on.

I took the window seat and gripped the armrest like it owed me a refund- every kilometre ahead already charging interest.

. . .

CityLink blurred past billboards- **NBN FASTER THAN GOSSIP**, a Vegemite jar flexing steroid biceps. Inside my chest, a second engine ran the numbers:

₹ 1,50,000 airfare

possible A$ 413 fine

– suitcase

– two jars pickle

= insolvency

I pictured my bag still orbiting Kuala Lumpur, chilli fumes drafting beagles for a war I'd already lost before touchdown.

———

Southern Cross → Thomastown

Myki machine swallowed twenty dollars, spat a blue card, left me broke but legitimate.

Platform 10 exhaled-Melbourne trains whisper where Indian ones shout.

I counted stations like *Amma's* prayer beads: Northcote, Croxton, Preston-each stop a reminder: clothes in limbo, lie in Customs, hope on credit. Reservoir graffiti read FAKE MILK. Fair; I was fake certainty in borrowed denim.

· · ·

Thomastown platform: gum leaves, cigarette butts, and a wind that smelled of wet eucalyptus and daring. The claim slip flapped in my pocket like a parking ticket for optimism.

I stepped off like a man returning to a city he hadn't yet arrived in-visa-stamped, overdressed, and already behind on belonging.

23 Cactus Court, Thomastown, Victoria: brick veneer bleached to the colour of abandoned promises. Chain-link gate listing like it had given up on verticality.

Door opened before I knocked.

Gaurav Gupta- bare feet, accountant's smile.

"Arjun? Flight okay? Must be tired." Two hospitable beats; then business:

"Rent A$ 110, bills twenty, bond two weeks. Cash better; transfer fine."

The room: bed, floral mattress, plastic desk, one power point, fizzing faint sparks. A suitcase-shaped void that still believed in connecting flights.

"Kitchen that way," he said. "Communal shelf-label everything. Wi-Fi password's *rentfirst*."

He vanished to re-enter his Zoom grid.

————

Fluorescents hummed. Fridge door opened onto a senate of neon Post-its:

- **COFFEE-ASK - Sanjay.** He padded in, hoodie up, measured grounds on a scale like narcotics, nodded once, vanished.
- **Halal Shelf ↑ - Zainab.** Crimson hijab, earbuds glowing; she slid a Milo sachet toward me without looking.
- **Night-shift Meals, Do Not Move - Rishi.** Steel-capped boots, eyes the colour of unpaid wages; he checked the microwave timer, muttered "fourteen hours till clock-on," left.

Rules taped where friendship should be. I closed the fridge gently, sealing a treaty I hadn't signed. Each colour told you who mattered, and when.

————

Back in my room, I genuflected to **CACTUS-2G**, typed the sacred password, and the family thread lit up:

Amma: Room clean? Pillow good? Eat on time.

Achan: Library card. Study timetable forthwith.

I replied: Reached. Wi-Fi good. Bag delayed. Love.

· · ·

Omitted: the lie, the pickle, the Post-it parliament. Even the fridge knew its politics. I just hadn't learned the language yet.

————

House settled into shift-worker rhythm: microwave beep, tap drip, one muffled guitar chord. Somewhere behind a closed door, Ming- the Taiwanese roommate Gaurav mentioned- let out a single strangled sob, then silence. First-night etiquette: ignore, survive.

Mattress smelled of someone else's detergent. Ceiling stain shaped like the Indian Ocean loomed overhead. Between me and that stain floated kilometres of airline carpet, a beagle's nose, and a suitcase packed with everything I could least afford to lose.

Sleep arrived - thin as an airport blanket.

In the half-dream that followed, Customs opened my luggage, found the pickle, and slapped on their own Post-it:

CONFISCATED – PAY LATER.

I woke before the fine totalled.

Heart already converting rupees to dollars.

Outside, Thomastown wind rattled the gate like a calculator shaking down the night for change.

11 SIGNAL STENGTH

Morning in Cactus Court tasted like tap water and envy.

The pantry was a gallery of padlocked jars; the fridge, a wall of Post-its warning me off anything not wrapped in condensation.

With my suitcase MIA, I owned one pair of jeans, a toothbrush, and zero phone service.

Maslow would've redrawn his pyramid just for me. Base layer: Buy a SIM.

———

Thomastown Aldi:

A$ 2 mobile starter kits lounged beside imported okra - cardboard shouting *ACTIVATE IN MINUTES.*

· · ·

Checkout scanned: A$ 2.

Utopia, so far.

Exit bench. Wi-Fi. Activation page. Fine print:

• Australian photo ID - **nope**

• Aussie credit card - **Visa-debit in rupees, declined**

• Utility bill - **belongs to Gaurav (and his poker debt)**

Screen blinked: **Error CF-05.**

Migration Rule #1:

Cheap always comes stapled to impossible.

Next stop: 7-Eleven Thomastown.

Neon glowed like a moral warning: **UNLIMITED OZ + 5 GB INTL – A$ 60 PRE-PAID**.

Clerk took my passport, asked for a bill. I shrugged.

He lowered his voice. "Cash and passport'll do. The system just needs something."

Sixty bucks-half a week's rent-slid across.

Plastic SIM slid back like a losing scratchie.

Change left: **A$ 24.**

. . .

I bought rice, two cans of tuna, the cheapest instant coffee unclaimed by Sanjay's Post-it empire.

Groceries fit in one hand. Shame needed both.

Hunger was manageable. Humiliation, less so.

Even my receipt blushed — all staples, no comfort.

Outside, three activation spins and-miracle-**4G lit up**, small as mercy.

Airport desk picked up on ring five.

"Good timing — your bag arrived from Kuala Lumpur this morning."

Relief punched a hole in my ribs. For one breath, I thought the curse had lifted — then the fine print kicked down the door.

"Held by Biosecurity — scanner flagged undeclared food. Collect in person, Freight Road. Open till six."

SkyBus fare. Inspection fee. Half-day lost.

I didn't even own the numbers yet and bureaucracy was already filling invoices.

· · ·

Migration Rule #2:

Every solved problem hides a commute.

————

Share-house kitchen: Zainab diced onions, Sanjay guarded his macro scale, Rishi snored off a night shift.

I labelled my brand-new instant coffee, stuck the Post-it on, tried not to read anyone else's neon commandments as prophecy.

Floral mattress. No suitcase. SIM finally alive.

My phone glowed signal strength.

Biosecurity's text pulsed louder:

Collect before 6:00 p.m. or storage fees apply.

————

4:12 p.m.

Phone buzzed again-**Roy Joseph**.

Roy: *"Number received. Address?"*

Achan must've passed it on already.

Pulse spiked, but I answered:

.   .   .

"Cactus Court, Thomastown. Room 3. Still finding my feet."

Silence. Then that ledger-tone:

"Feet or knees, da- both bend the same. First payment due in 24 sleeps. Clock doesn't mind the time zone."

Click.

———

Screen returned to home.

4G bars still bright, as if good news were possible.

Outside, the Thomastown wind rattled the chain-link like a calculator shaking coins.

Inside, I watched the minutes tick down until Biosecurity closed- and pictured a jar of garlic pickle sweating in quarantine, **interest accruing even on nostalgia.**

12 TICK NOW, PAY LATER

Thomastown, Friday, 17 February 2017

6:55 a.m. - Thomastown Station

Wet eucalyptus drips onto the platform roof, its resin tang mingling with hot-metal rail dust. Commuters queue like coins in a fare gate: dusty work polos, chipped coffee cups, impatient perfume.

I stand outside their currency, backpack straps biting through yesterday's deodorant.

Some scroll real estate listings like escape plans. Others blast Punjabi hits into one AirPod and elevator music into the other — the kind that chases endless floors and never quite arrives.

.   .   .

Two trains and a SkyBus: ninety minutes of travel, so a jar of chilli could keep its visa.

Migration rule #3:

A lie costs a day out of your future.

7:42 a.m. - Southern Cross ⟶ Tullamarine

SkyBus ticket: **A\$ 22**. Driver bantered about half-price roses, full-price traffic.

I checked my wallet: **A\$ 196** to my name.

8:18 a.m. - Freight Road Quarantine Depot

Bunker behind cargo hangars, windows dark as grudges.

Officer Stein-badge 404- pulled my suitcase forward.

"Open it, please."

Zipper rasped. Two factory-sealed garlic-pickle jars blinked in the light.

"Card says no food, Mr Nair."

"Cultural condiment," I tried.

.   .   .

"Undeclared food is a quarantine offence," she replied, voice non-negotiable.

Printer spat out an invoice: **Inspection Fee A$ 90**.

Balance after swipe: **A$ 106**.

"Next time, tick *yes*," she said, sliding the jars back.

I nodded, throat tasting of vinegar and shame.

9:40 a.m. - Airport Food Court

Flat white: **A$ 5**- rent on a plastic chair.

Departure boards rolled through cities I could no longer afford.

Phone buzzed-**Roy**.

Address received. Proud of you, da. Stay focused.

Pride at three per cent monthly interest.

11:12 a.m. - Return Loop

SkyBus rattled the day's numbers into my spine:

.   .   .

Expense A$

Airport bus (return) 22

Phone SIM top-up 60

Groceries 12

Local buses 22

Quarantine fine 90

Left to breathe 106

Driver glanced back. "Bag all clear now, mate?"

"Quarantined and released."

"Welcome to the ecosystem."

Ecosystem: where rules and roots favour the ones already planted.

Lesson noted. Photosynthesis required-immediately.

13 NAMES, BUTCHERED

Melbourne, Monday, 20 February 2017

University Orientation Day.

"Ah-roooon... Ur-jin?"

The tutor's eyebrows contracted like they'd found a war crime hidden in the roll sheet.

Twenty students, one firing squad of unfamiliar vowels; my name, **Arjun Ajith Nair**, stood at attention before it could be executed a fourth time.

I raised a hand.

.   .   .

"Here. *Ar-jun*-short *u*, rhymes with **fun**."

She produced that imported Australian grin-part apology, part empire souvenir.

"Thanks, **Ar-jurn**."

Close enough for horseshoes, grenades, and linguistic deforestation.

———

Building 80, Level 7 - Tutorial Room 10

White box breathing refrigerated optimism. Posters barked **INNOVATE · COLLABORATE · DISRUPT**-verbs on anabolic steroids.

My A$ 60 pre-paid SIM already wheezed at the campus login page: username, password, mother's maiden blood type.

Ice-breaker round: name, origin, one *fun* fact.

• **Lexie**, Geelong, surfs with her pug.

• **Nikolai**, Russian-Aussie, DJs drum-and-bass on Twitch.

My turn.

"**Arjun**, Kerala, south-west India. Fun fact..."

Killing a man isn't tutorial-safe; owing an A$ 90 pickle tax isn't fun.

"...I cook fish curry that tastes like monsoon."

Polite nods. One genuine *yum*.

Tutor tilted her head. "Kerala- that's near Goa?"

"Two states south. Coastal. Lots of rain and inconvenient literacy."

She scribbled whatever translation fit her atlas: **fish + rain**.

―――

Orientation Booth B

Fluorescent judgment behind a plastic desk. Volunteer laminated my identity onto cardstock:

Name: Arjun Ajith Nair

ID: 1046257

Preferred: Arj (his idea)

.   .   .

"All good, **Ar-jin**?" Attempt number four. The ID froze my face mid-grimace-bureaucracy timing its punchline.

————

Federation Square Queue

Barista scrawled **RJ** on the lid and yelled,

"Flat white for **Urgent!**"

No takers. "**Origen!**"

We locked eyes. I rescued the cup, wondering how many wrong names equal a legal alias.

The cup wasn't mine, but the mistake felt familiar enough to answer to.

Outside, spring flirted with wind chill. I dispatch- proofed my existence to the family WhatsApp:

Officially enrolled. Bought A$ 12 coffee & union fee. ROI pending.

Amma replied instantly: "Spell name properly. Eat fruit."

Achan, ever practical: "Roy Jacob called- wants Aussie number again. Don't delay, *mon*."

· · ·

Campus Wi-Fi 404'd. Technology charges foreign-transaction fees in patience.

———

Workshop - Own Your Narrative

Consultant in blazer-sneakers begged for volunteers. I stood.

"I'm **Arjun- rhymes with sun**. Background in code, foreground in uncertainty. Elevator pitch? I build bridges out of yesterday's mistakes before tomorrow collapses."

Polite applause. Consultant beamed like I'd notarised his TED Talk outline.

———

Tram Home

Myki reader chirped **WELCOME ARJUN**- first system all day to get it right. Fare A$ 4.60, validation priceless.

———

Cactus Court Kitchen - 8:07 p.m.

.   .   .

Fluorescent fatigue, reheated-Maggi haze. Rice cooker empty; tuna it is- again.

Hallway soundtrack:

Zainab (low, sharp): "You never ask how my shift went."

Kartik (half Tamil, half surrender): "Z, deadlines. Talk after exam, okay?"

Click. Silence. Post-it parliament hadn't listed *tension* as a shared commodity.

Phone buzzed mid-tuna. *Achan*:

Roy still waiting. Send a number or he'll ring the pharmacy next.

Typed *Soon, Acha*. Deleted. Typed *Tomorrow*. Sent.

Rice cooker beeped to announce emptiness; fridge light died; somewhere,

a phone sobbed in Mandarin.

My tongue still burned from mispronounced coffee, but at least "**Ar-jun**" echoed correctly inside my own skull.

· · ·

Groceries, textbooks, corridor diplomacy- tomorrow's quests.

Tonight, I shut the kitchen door, letting mysteries marinate with the Maggi smell.

One syllable at a time, I reminded myself.

One room, one rent, one name- if I can keep it.

14 LAUNDRY SAMOSAS

Hey- quick question before the shift eats you: when exactly did we first meet? Was it the laundrette on Station Street? The smell of Surf and steam keeps replaying, but memory is a pickpocket. All I'm sure of is detergent, fluorescent headache, and you wrestling a beige monster that tried to eat your arm.

———

5.30 p.m

I woke to the unmistakable scent of someone else's life - mystery cologne, old detergent, homesick sweat - baked deep into the floral bedsheet Gaurav called "fresh-ish."

After six nights, I called it ambience. On the tenth, I called it a biohazard.

. . .

I stripped the sheet, rolled it with my single towel, and headed to Station Street's coin laundry - two blocks past the kebab shop selling last night's chicken as today's bargain.

Thomastown Laundrette

Surf, steam, and hot metal. Four washing machines crouched like slot machines with bad odds. A laminated sign warned:

NO DYING PETS OR DUVETS. (Comma scrubbed out by history.)

Ten bucks into the dispenser got me four grimy tokens.

I loaded the sheet, towel, and the T-shirt I'd worn three times through three storms.

Enter: the doona.

She wrangled it through the door like it owed her rent - a king-size beige beast halfway up her arm.

I grabbed a corner and tugged.

"Need a spare elbow?"

. . .

She smiled - fast, cautious.

"Appreciated," she said.

Accent: Nepali vowels, sitcom consonants.

Hair twisted up, except one streak that bounced every time she yanked the doona.

Her: "Rekha. Part-time student, full-time doona wrangler."

Me: "Arjun. Full-time student, part-time sheet exorcist."

Coins clanked. Machines groaned.

We claimed two cracked plastic chairs, front row to the spin cycle.

We swapped the usuals.

Course?

• *Her:* Dropped nursing for pastry. "Less blood, more butter."

• *Me:* MBA detour via debt. "Management by anxiety."

Family?

• Her: Kathmandu father. No mention of a mother.

• Me: Kerala everything. Too much to explain.

Fun facts?

• She can fold a sari in 45 seconds. "Timed by aunties."

• I once coded a cricket scoreboard that "accidentally" ignored the other team's runs.

It ran glitch-free. Morally questionable.

The vending machine rattled like it was keeping score - and for once, neither of us flinched.

She glanced at her Coles receipt.

I flashed my A$ 8 laundry stub.

Her: "Laundry tax."

Me: "Price of smelling like yourself."

Her: "Or not smelling like the last tenant."

Me: "Exactly. Sheet exorcism."

When the washers stopped, she hugged her doona like a familiar enemy. I retrieved my sheet - finally smelling like detergent, not ghosts.

·   ·   ·

Me: "You picnic on your bed?"

Her: "Less lonely than a table for one."

Me: "Next time pick a park. I'll bring plates."

Her: "Op-shop porcelain."

Me: "Done."

We shook on it. No paperwork.

She tapped my A$ 60 SIM into her cracked phone.

My pocket buzzed - first contact stored by someone who wasn't a debt collector or Roy.

———

Outside the laundrette, we parted at the corner.

Her: "Thanks for the elbow."

Me: "Thanks for the laugh."

———

I walked home with the sheet warm in my arms, practising what the air had smelled like - eucalyptus, steam, something new.

• • •

Maybe it wasn't a meet-cute.

Maybe just laundry.

But the warmth stayed - even after the machines went quiet.

15 CAFFEINE TAX

Kitchen

The fridge coughs its last breath just as **Sanjay** erupts:

"Who finished my *Bru Gold*?"

He waves the jar like court evidence- Post-it half-torn, granules below yesterday's line.

Zainab freezes over cornflakes; **Rishi** mutters, grave-yard thieves steal cash, not caffeine.

Kartik- fresh from Zainab's room, chain still winking- gives an innocent shrug.

Sanjay's glare lands on the only untested shelf-mate: me, the new Malayalee in yesterday's rupee-priced jeans.

. . .

"Has to be you. South-Indian types never respect shelves."

Coffee breath, caste after-taste.

———

Interrogation

Sanjay: "You dip?"

Me: "No."

Sanjay: "Lie once, pay twice. Your sort freeloads."

Me: "'My sort'?"

Sanjay: "Kerala, Tamil-same curry, same trespass."

I smiled, the kind that carries no teeth—just survival.

Kartik stays shirtless; Rishi disappears to "get ready."

Zainab grips her mug, bracing for collateral.

The fridge hummed like it had heard this argument before.

Sanjay leans in. "Bru Gold isn't charity, brother. Pay-

-or relocate your poverty."

11:12 a.m. - Servo

Last ten dollars buys a new jar and bread tough enough to bruise morals.

Receipt prints like a minor conviction.

Back home, I tape the jar to Sanjay's door:

REPLACED - ARJUN

No apology- just settlement.

———

Sanjay prowls once, jar cradled; silence heavier than shouting.

Jar reappears on the fridge, Post-it upgraded: **PRIVATE • TOUCH = FINE**-yellow square, black threat.

Hierarchy has shelving.

———

Running Ledger

Wallet start A$ 111

– Bru restitution 10

Float left A$ 101

Rent looms, Biosecurity still wants its pickle fee, Roy keeps pinging for my postcode, and now the house levies a coffee tax.

Australia keeps lengthening the declaration form.

Instant tea tastes of cardboard and compliance.

Migration Rule #4:

Peace is prepaid in humiliations.

Outside, Woolton Avenue shakes gossip into the gutters; inside, the tube light flickers like a guilty conscience.

I text nothing to *Amma* - mothers sniff debt through silence.

Mask on, head down, tribute paid. Coffee jar, pickle fine, tuition - same equation, darker variables.

One spoon at a time, the balance tilts; one day it will snap.

1:03 p.m. – Laundry Line

Karthik finds me by the backyard, pretending to sort socks that don't match.

"Hey... You alright?"

He doesn't sit. Just leans against the fence like it might help him stay upright.

"I've had worse interrogations," I say. "Not the first time Bru Gold became casteist contraband."

He huffs a dry laugh. "He's a dick. You didn't deserve that."

I squint at him. "You and Zainab okay?"

He runs a hand through his hair. Shrugs. Eyes somewhere near the washing line.

"I don't know what I'm doing, man. Back home, it was simple: study, succeed, don't embarrass the family. No one told me what to do in between. Zainab made it feel less like I was on pause."

I nod. Not sure if it's permission or pity.

"I'll go back eventually," he says. "Marry whoever my parents pick. I know that. But right now? I don't know how to want anything safe."

I tap my mug. Instant tea, cooling fast.

"Some of us were never taught safe," I say. "Just silence."

The socks on the line twist in the wind - a mismatched pair, still trying to dry.

16 REPUBLIC OF PORTABLE COMFORT

Princes Park, Sunday, 12 March 2017

Cut grass and liniment drift over the oval. Carlton reserves rehearse another loss.

Rekha sits on the hillside, doona spread like a low flag nobody salutes.

I arrive carrying two op-shop plates wrapped in the half-written essay I've been dodging.

"Welcome to the Republic of Portable Comfort," she says, kicking off her shoes.

The grass stains her heel, but she doesn't flinch—like softness is something she's still learning to unlearn.

. . .

Lunch stash

- Two *samosas* sweating through paper

- A Tupperware of *pulissery* that's seen better microwaves

- A 75-cent Aldi baguette pretending to be fusion

I set one rose-pattern plate beside her sun-bleached Olympic souvenir.

"Chip matches my attendance," I joke.

"At least the plate shows up," she says, tearing the baguette in half.

She's quieter today. Eyes on the sky.

"Do you ever think we're wasting our time down here?"

"Sometimes," I say. "But the alternative is drowning somewhere else."

She nods.

"Eat. Cheaper than therapy."

We trade flood stories:

Her aunt's motel in Pokhara.

My father's pharmacy in Kottayam.

Neither insured. Both still standing.

We lie back on the doona, heads just touching.

Quick-fire trivia:

• Biggest fear? "Ticket inspectors."

• Secret skill? "Naming every visa subclass like a rap verse."

• Word you miss most? She whispers a Nepali syllable I can't spell.

I offer *kanji*. Malayalam rice porridge. The food of homesick teeth.

A gust flips the doona. My phone pings the corner - screen lit up with her laundrette grin.

"Delete if creepy."

"Evidence," I reply.

She snaps a photo of the plates.

"Mutual incrimination," she says.

Her phone buzzes.

A draft text lights up: **Mom?**

(*The one she hadn't mentioned.*)

She pockets it before it decides what to do.

Stadium lights clack on. Shadows shift.

"Same time in two weeks?"

"Same plates," I say.

She gives a half-smile.

"Maybe real cutlery. If the café roster stops ghosting me."

She deserves warmth. All I have is weather.

11:00 p.m. – Cactus Court

Rose plate shelved.

Photo archived.

The house feels like a hostel auditioning for permanence.

Ming's door clicks. One sob, then silence.

Possums rattle the bins. The fridge hums like a tired witness.

I open the park photo. Type:

Survived the day. Plate intact. You?

Delete.

She has an early shift.

Outside, the house holds its breath.
Inside, for now, so do we.

17 SUGAR SHELF DIPLOMACY

Rekha had started showing up in Thomastown more often enough for Zainab to stop announcing her, and for Sanjay to start clearing a stool on laundry day.

Sometimes she'd stay the night, crash on Zainab's doona fortress, or commandeer the kitchen to fix chai that tasted like Nepali weather and low-grade defiance.

Sometimes she'd disappear halfway through a sentence.

No one asked why.

Sanjay found us both at the kitchen table - me re-labelling my coffee jar with deliberate overkill, Rekha flicking through someone's battered *Women's Weekly*.

. . .

He hovered by the microwave, cleared his throat.

"I, uh-" He didn't look at me.

"I overreacted. That Bru Gold thing. It wasn't... right."

Rekha's eyebrows lifted just enough to let him know she'd heard.

Sanjay scratched his neck. "I miss home. I think that's why I grip things too hard. Jars, routines. Even Post-its. They feel like proof someone's listening."

He didn't wait for a reply. Just tapped the fridge, then added, "Yours is the only coffee that doesn't taste like burnt cardboard, anyway."

Then he left - the fridge door swinging half-closed, apology still hanging in the steam above the rice cooker.

Rekha didn't comment.

Just reached over, dipped a spoon into my jar, and stirred her mug.

"Don't let it go to your head," she said. "He's still going to blame you when the fridge leaks."

. . .

Later, she lingered at the table, scrolling her phone like it owed her answers.

"You okay?" I asked.

"I have to go to Sydney for a bit. Family," she said - vague as checkout small talk.

Then, quieter: "I don't want to talk about it. Just... don't ask, okay?"

"Okay."

Mood folded in her shoulders like origami gone wrong.

She left before dinner, her mug in the sink - unwashed, but angled toward the drain, like an intention half-kept.

———

Back then, I didn't know how to unpick your moods.

I still don't know if I'm meant to.

Sometimes I want to tell you I'm attracted to you - like, *really* - but I'm anxious of the ghosts you walk with.

You never name them.

And I don't know what it means to love someone without a torch.

That night, after you told me about the Sydney trip, I lay back on the floral mattress and listened to the Thomastown wind rattle the gutters like it was trying to decode all our silences at once.

18 SIRENS & SHADOWS

Thomastown, Wednesday, 16 August 2017

6.10 a.m.

Red strobes sliced the hallway.

Paramedics floated past unpaid rent notices.

Ming, still breathing, barely disappeared under Velcro straps and soft apologies.

Door slam. Siren. Silence.

———

7:43 a.m. – Laundry-Shed Concrete

Rekha crouched outside the shed. Hoodie up. Eyes fixed on the laundry steam like it owed her a memory.

. . .

Bathroom light lit a perfect rectangle behind her. She sat just outside it, like light had a price tag.

I didn't speak. Just sat beside her. We watched a line of ants cross the concrete like they had nowhere to be and all day to get there.

She nodded at Ming's window.

"Minds crack quietly, don't they?"

I nodded back.

She turned her phone in her palm. Switched it off. Turned it on. Switched it off again. Then, finally, I spoke.

"He wasn't even my real uncle. Just came around too much."

Pause.

"Mum ran when I was eight. Motel in Pokhara. Sixteen rooms. Vacuum-sealed smiles."

She kept her voice level. Like reading out charges she'd already served time for.

. . .

"Grandmother ran the register. Aunts did linen.

Then Dev moved in 'to help.' Stayed to hunt."

A beat.

"First 'lesson' - behind Reception. English practice. Open your mouth wider."

Another beat.

"Second lesson - no camera working that day."

She didn't cry. She chewed her nail until it split.

"Grandmother needed his loan. Aunts looked away.

You know how it is - reputation pays the electricity bill."

The silence stretched. No more ants. No wind.

Then she said it like a punchline:

"He's in Sydney now. Migration agent. Prints student visas like ID cards."

She laughed. Dry.

"Suggested Melbourne so he could 'keep an eye on me.' I picked it so a highway could keep him off me."

I asked, quietly, "Police?"

She scoffed.

"Predators don't need alibis. They collect them in advance."

Wind slapped the shed door; she flinched, then steadied.

"I watched Ming fold. Dev bends people the same way - slow, then snap."

———

I wanted to say something smart. Or kind. Or useful.

Instead, I said:

"We break him first."

She looked at me, not for comfort, but for verification.

Then nodded once.

We split a stale croissant. No butter. No sweetness. Just something warm to hold.I didn't say anything at the time - just listened.

But this is why I wrote it down.

Not to preserve it.

To make sure it doesn't go back into silence.

Because you never told me the full thing again.

Not like that.

You tucked it back behind sarcasm and shifts and playlists and croissants.

And I didn't ask.

But I remembered everything.

How you flinched at doors.

How you scanned for exits in every café.

How the air changed when anyone said "family."

You told me enough.

Now it's here. Not so you have to read it.

Just so you don't have to carry all of it alone anymore.

19 STRAIGHT LINES. SHARP TURNS.

Just past midnight

The kitchen was dark except for the soft whirr of the fridge and the blue tick of the microwave clock. I went in for water. Found Zainab already there.

She was perched on the window ledge, barefoot, hoodie draped over her shoulders, hijab long gone for the night. Hair still damp from a shower. She didn't flinch when I entered - just lifted her chin like I was expected.

"You need the stove?" she asked, voice low.

"Nope. Just thirsty."

. . .

I poured water, leaned on the counter. She tapped her phone twice, then turned the screen off. The room felt strangely mutual - like we were on a shift neither of us had agreed to but neither wanted to end.

———

"Karthik asleep?" I asked.

"Eventually."

She smirked. "He had a lot of feelings about soup."

I snorted. "Soup is political in this house."

She didn't laugh, just took a slow sip from her mug.

"He thinks we're serious," she said. "I think he's sweet."

That was Zainab.

Straight lines. Sharp turns.

———

"You okay?" I asked. The question felt too round in my mouth. Too big.

. . .

She tilted her head. "I mean... define okay."

I didn't answer. She filled the silence instead.

"Some days I feel like I'm finally living. Like, actually choosing things. My clothes, my work, who I sleep with."

Pause.

"Then sometimes I open my class WhatsApp group and see a photo of my cousin's engagement party back in Penang and wonder if I'm just a blur in someone else's cautionary tale."

———

She looked at me then. Really looked.

"You ever feel like that? Like you're the footnote version of yourself?"

I nodded. "Only on Tuesdays and weekends."

She smiled, tired and toothless. "I keep thinking I should care less."

. . .

"You don't strike me as someone who cares what people think."

"I don't," she said. "Until I do."

———

Silence again. Not awkward. Just tired.

She tapped her mug twice. "Wei's coming over tomorrow. Not staying. Just... coming over."

She didn't owe me the detail, but I heard the weight in the offering. Wei - her classmate. The other one.

"I like them different," she added. "Karthik wants me to meet his sister. Wei won't even tag me in memes."

I laughed, gently. "Luxury problems."

"Survival tactics," she corrected.

———

She stood then. Pulled her hoodie back over her head. Pinned her hair in one practised twist.

· · ·

"I don't want to go home yet," she said. "But I don't think I want to be here forever either."

I didn't say anything. Some truths didn't need echoing.

She padded to the hallway barefoot, stopped at the edge of the light.

"For what it's worth," she said, "you're one of the few boys here who doesn't look like he's auditioning for something."

Then she left, and the hallway swallowed her up.

20 PEDAL PANIC

I'd been balancing everything - studies, shifts, rent, and Roy.

On paper, I was doing okay. Assignments submitted, attendance 82%, interest paid on time.

Roy got his ₹18,000 every month like clockwork, and I got to breathe - barely. Between 7-Eleven stints and group project debates about leadership models we'd never be allowed to practice.

But then Roy changed the rules.

. . .

No explanation. No missed payment. Just a message with revised terms:

New rate: 4.5% per month. Backpay due. Penalty interest for "delays in processing."

He dressed it up in legalese and politeness - the kind that sounds professional until you remember he still has our land deed and *Amma's* bangles as collateral.

I'd borrowed honestly. I was repaying honestly.

But Roy wasn't in the honesty business - he was in the addiction-to-hope business.

Every extension came with a catch. Every "grace period" was retroactively charged.

Migration Rule #5:

Debt doesn't forgive; it escalates.

I called Roy. He said things like *"standard adjustment"* and *"rates need to reflect current exposure."*

When I asked what changed, he said:

"Your timeline, da. You're running late."

. . .

As if life were an exam and he held the invigilator's watch.

Then came the WhatsApp video call.

Incoming: *Achan*

The screen lit up with his face, dimmed by the single bulb behind him.

"*Mon* - listen. Roy's men came."

His voice was low, clipped like someone off-camera could hear him.

"Two months' interest. ₹36,000. Fourteen days. They said next visit won't be this polite."

The call ended.

No lecture. No blessing.

Just the ceiling fan clicking like it's keeping score.

Wallet: A$ 11.80 and *Amma's* gold chain- the only heirloom in my zip pocket. The chain hums with the hope she packed into my departure photo, belief melted into nine carats.

I weighed it in my palm, not for value, but to remember what desperation should never cost.

———

10:42 - High Street, Preston

Cash Converters breathes recycled despair. The kind that smells like burnt toast and pawned intentions.

I place the chain on the scale. Already know its weight.

"Nine-carat, 4.3 grams. Three-ten if you pawn, two-eighty if you sell."

Three-ten buys Roy a week. Costs *Amma* a lifetime promise.

I close my hand around it. Pocket the chain. Desperation postponed, just for today.

I double back. The ledger won't balance without sacrifice.

This time, I place the chain on the counter and leave it there.

Pawned, not sold. Faith put on hold.

———

11:35 - Melbourne Plasma Centre

Poster yells EARN UP TO A$ 400 A MONTH over smiling blondes in bandages.

Clipboard nurse scans my visa, frowns.

"Need Medicare number and six-month residency. Only Aussie or NZ donors today, sorry."

Apparently, the lucky country doesn't need my brown blood. Just my green bills.

Migration Rule #6:

Charity pays in the dominant pigment.

———

22:15 - Cactus Court Lounge

Telegram pings: Rishi

FOOTSCRAY RUN • TONIGHT •A$ 200 CASH • NEED RIDER • BRING BIKE

Two hundred is oxygen. Morals are elective.

Inventory:

Cash: A$ 11.80

Bike: 0

Chain: Pawned

Debt: A$ 870 AUD

———

22:46 - Begging for Wheels

• Gaurav's Uber fixie? Flat tyres.

• Kartik? Locked in with Zainab.

• Marketplace bikes live in Geelong - might as well be Narnia.

DM from Wei- Zainab's quiet orbit:

"Blue Giant, cage #37 Carlton. Deposit A$ 50. Break = buy."

Groceries fund bleeds into PayID. Address received. Morals mortgaged.

———

23:54 - Carlton Underground

Rust-flaked Giant. Helmet still warm with someone else's sweat.

Lock snaps: complicity notarised in steel.

———

00:04 a.m. - Nicholson Street

Tyres squeal. Wind cuts like unpaid rent.

My legs haven't pedalled in months. Thighs scream. Brakes whisper nothing.

A Corolla turns too close- mirror misses my shoulder by two inches. Rider down the road yells, "Watch it, bro!" Not at me. Just the air.

Bike jolts over a tram groove. Chain skips. Heart hammers louder than the pedals.

Up ahead: red and blue flash in a rearview mirror.

Cop car idles at the roundabout, bored into their shift. One glance at my high-vis jacket, courier bag, and brown skin.

They look through me.

I'm an international student. I'm invisible until something breaks.

I ride on. Legs stiff, jaw tighter. Morals: shaken, not stirred.

———

00:21 a.m. - Barkly St, Footscray

Night-manager's tats read MALICE in Gothic.

"No cops. Forty minutes. Deliver. Don't open."

Then, with a smirk that tastes like bleach:

"Curry-run special, yeah? Don't spill the turmeric."

Grey satchel. Vacuum-sealed. Lighter than guilt, heavier than law.

Drop-pin: Chinatown alley. A$ 200 on delivery.

Job Card:

Distance: 12 km

Time limit: 40 min

Bike health: 45% brakes, 0% lights

Package: Felony (probable)

———

1:11 a.m. - Chinatown

Honda Jazz idles. Rear door cracks. Gloved hand grabs satchel, tosses two crisp hundreds.

Bleach stings the air-sanitiser for conscience.

———

2:04 a.m. - Cage #37

Bike re-chained. Deposit safe-if ethics let Wei refund it.

———

2:39 a.m. - Cactus Court Hallway

Phone buzzes.

Rekha: Where are you?

Ignored.

———

2:55 a.m. - Cactus Court Kitchen

Rain-soaked notes: A$ 200. Roy's meter still snarls.

48-HOUR SPRINT

Run | Package | Pay | Running Total

#1 | Footscray pills | A$ 200 |A $ 211.80

#2 | Brunswick "freight" | A$ 300 | A$ 511.80

#3 | St Kilda metal case | A$ 350 | A$ 861.80

Bike chain snaps after run #3.

. . .

I drag its carcass through alleys while dawn bleeds across the pavement.

Adrenaline buzzes like a dodgy plug.

———

8:20 a.m. - Brunswick Backstreet

Last-minute job ping. Package marked "SPECIAL ART SUPPLIES."

Delivery window: thirty minutes.

No questions, no names. Just A$ 40 in an envelope and a can of Solo as tip.

Enough to push me out of red and into the pawnshop.

———

9:15 a.m. - Coburg Milk Bar (Side Run)

Another ping: FRAGILE – URGENT.

White box wrapped in brown tape, sender won't meet my eyes.

. . .

Drop-off is a poker lounge near Sunshine.

Half the trip is uphill. I pedal like my debt is on fire.

Thirty-seven minutes later, I arrive dripping.

Receiver nods, peels off A$ 320.

Tip: a mint and a wink, I don't unwrap.

T-10 d 06 h - Ledger

Cash on hand: A$ 901.80 + A$ 320 = A$ 1,221.80

Debt target: ≈ A$ 870

Surplus: A$ 351.80

Gold chain: ready to reclaim.

Plasma: still off-limits.

Legs: broken but paid.

Faith, bought back with adrenaline, guilt, and four nights of borrowed morality.

It held, but like cheap thread—tight, fraying, one pull from unravelling.

———

10:08 a.m. - Pawnshop Return

I hand the clerk A$ 310 and repurchase *Amma's* chain, twenty-four hours before interest compounds.

He stamps REDEEMED.

The receipt feels like forgiveness. The chain, like breath.

———

11:29 a.m. - Wire Transfer

₹ 36,000 → Roy Jacob.

WhatsApp ticks blue.

Roy: "Good boy. Clock resets."

For now.

———

Screen lights again.

Rekha - no words. Just a screenshot.

Dev (-61) 4:11 a.m.

"Landing MEL tomorrow. Room booked Grey St, St Kilda. Swing by day after- need to 'catch up' with my favourite niece. 🫤"

. . .

Her caption below it. Six keystrokes that rattle harder than sirens:

SCARED.

21 DROPBOX GOSPEL

Grey Street, St Kilda. Wikipedia calls it a red-light corridor.

Locals say: Don't walk alone.

My stomach just calls it *prelude*.

The kind of postcode that digests migrant girls and belches silence.

Dev's listing: Airbnb. *Urban Chic Studio - Self Check-In - No Parties.*

Door code: #2310. The same number he sent Rekha.

The same location that makes my hands itch.

·   ·   ·

7:18 p.m. – Route 96, Swanston to Fitzroy

The tram moves like it's dodging memory.

Neon VACANCY signs blink like dying stars.

A girl with too much eyeliner stares at her reflection, trying to remember which lie she told last.

Dev is already a verb on this street.

You can feel it in the oil stains, the flickering porch lights, the way the city flinches around him.

8:02 p.m. – Gumption Café, Opposite #48 Grey Street

$2.80 flat white - moral camouflage.

Laptop angled so the screen reflects the Airbnb entrance.

8:37 p.m. – Same View

Dev steps out. Hair still greasy from yesterday.

Shirt clinging to sweat like guilt.

Behind him: a girl who could be Rekha's reflection - if you scraped off a year and dialled up the fear.

No bag. No voice. Just hoodie, hunched shoulders, and compliance.

They slide into a silver Mazda. Like it's a carpool. Like it's routine.

Day Two – Same Café, New Girl

School uniform this time. Eyes like locked doors.

My coffee goes cold beside me, untouched.

The screen stays live - camera lens taped into a disposable cup lid.

Feed uploading to my burner cloud.

Not evidence yet - just proof the world works exactly as she feared.

Same hoodie. Smaller frame. No eye contact.

She knew the routine. That's what broke me.

Day Three – 10:46 a.m. – Bunnings Warehouse

$89 surveillance rig: fake charger cam, fake uniform, real towel stack.

Morality left behind in aisle four next to discount rope.

No receipt.

· · ·

11:08 a.m. – Grey Street, #48

Knock once.

Enter like I've done it before.

The air tastes like deodoriser sprayed over shame.

Sink smells of ramen and bleach.

Charger-cam behind the TV. Blink. Adjust. Angle. Exit.

11:04 p.m. – Room 3B, Cactus Court

Cloud feed pings. Motion detected.

Dev.

Girl. Hoodie. Vodka in a Disney mug.

Mattress. Stillness. His laugh.

Her silence is louder.

11:26 p.m. – Rekha

Text: *Dev postponed. Said he's busy with guests. Can we meet tomorrow? I'm scared.*

. . .

I type: *Stay away.*

Delete.

Type again: *Okay. Text me when you get there.*

Send.

I stare at the screen long after it goes dark.

What I just saw isn't new.

Not to her. Not to him.

Maybe not even to me.

———

I remember what you told me.

Not everything — just enough to identify the shape.

Like a weapon outlined under cloth.

It comes in pieces.

Not a story. A pattern.

He never asked. He hovered.

Near chai trays. Near migration desks.

He waited.

And when you didn't give, he said *difficult.*

Then offered to help.

They didn't call him a predator.

They called him *Dev Mama.*

The visa guy.

The respectable one.

He never rushed.

He moved around the edges.

Didn't stalk. Just stayed.

Didn't grope. Just touched — flat, casual, deniable.

Long enough to register.

Short enough to survive cross-examination.

You told me once —

At a wedding.

You leaned forward with chai.

He placed a hand between your ribs and spine.

You kept smiling. Then you stopped breathing.

That was enough.

.   .   .

He never used the word.

He used synonyms.

Confidence.

Exposure.

Mentorship.

He told your family you were *smart.*

He told you *Melbourne isn't far.*

You never gave me the whole thing.

You didn't need to.

I've seen how you choose seats near exits.

How you pause before entering a room.

How your jaw tightens when men say your name too easily.

I remember enough.

That's why I printed the photo.

Why I taped the charger-cam behind the TV.

Why I'm writing this now.

.   .   .

Because men like him don't vanish.

They invoice.

They network.

They walk free.

But not today.

————

Day Four – The Blackmail

Print still-frame.

Dev's hand. A thigh. Timestamp burning like a scar.

Stuffed in an envelope with a burner number.

Message: **I KNOW WHAT YOU BUY IN ROOM #48. CALL BEFORE MIDNIGHT.**

7:18 p.m. – Grey Street, #48

I tape the envelope under the keypad. Hoodie up.

Café skipped. Appetite buried.

Back on the tram, the phone buzzes. Not Dev.

Roy.

A debt collector without morals lecturing me on time.

Interest has new rhythms now.

12:07 a.m. – Cactus Court

Private number.

Line opens. A voice like melted ghee spills into my ear.

Dev: "So. Mysterious caller. You forgot to sign your blackmail letter, brother?"

He tries to sound amused. The kind of amusement that costs A$ 300 per hour in immigration consultancy fees.

Me: "Didn't want to spoil the suspense."

Dev: "Ah! Very clever. Scriptwriter? Film school? Or just angry boy with Wi-Fi?"

He's trying to place the accent. Not because he cares - because men like him need to know where to file you. North Indian? South Indian? Dangerous? Disposable?

. . .

Me: "Don't worry about the accent. Worry about the girl in the grey hoodie."

Silence. That woke something.

Dev: "Who are you?"

Now the fun part. The crack in the teacup.

Me: "I'm nobody. But the kind of nobody who knows what timestamp your last guest arrived, and what school she missed the next morning."

Dev: "Okay, okay. So this is about that girl."

Fake sigh.

"You boys fall in love too easily. One girl says no and now you want to be hero."

Me: "Fifty thousand."

Dev: "What?"

Me: "Dollars. Not rupees. And you disappear."

Dev: "Disappear where? I live here, bhai. I pay taxes. I shake hands with MPs."

.   .   .

Me: "Then shake with your left hand. You'll need the right to carry the duffel."

He switches gears - smug to stern, like changing lanes without a blinker.

Dev: "You know who I am?"

Me: "Yes. And now you do too. A man one phone call away from being a headline."

Dev: "You students... always think one photo, one video, and the world will stop. You think your voice matters."

Me: "Not mine. Hers."

Now he's quiet. Not out of fear. Out of calculation. You can hear the Excel sheet loading in his head.

Dev: "So. You want money. To go away?"

Me: "No. I want you to go away. The money is just your apology to the rest of us for being allowed to walk this long."

. . .

Dev: "Where?"

Me: "Federation Square. Noon. Public. Drop the bag. Walk."

Dev: "And if I bring police?"

Me: "Then I send them the Dropbox link. And the timestamp. And the audio file where your voice says, 'You're very mature for sixteen.'"

Dev: "You won't do it."

Me: "Try me. I'm a student, remember? We've got nothing to lose and all day to queue."

Pause. Deep one.

He doesn't say yes.

But he doesn't say no either.

Dev: "Okay. Tomorrow. Bring umbrella. Might rain."

Click.

12:00 p.m. – Federation Square

.   .   .

He arrives five minutes late, which tells me two things:

1. He's scared.

2. He still thinks he's in charge.

Dev the Messiah. Patron Saint of Half-Filled Visa Forms. Migration's Middleman.

And yet, here he is - sweat blossoming through his armpits like poorly timed metaphors.

He scans the plaza like he's searching for a misplaced briefcase. What he's really searching for is *control*.

Control doesn't return his calls today.

He's dressed like a consultant trying to impress a Tinder date: slim-fit shirt two sizes too small, sunglasses that cost more than the girls he traffics in fake promises, and a duffel bag slung like he's heading to a yoga retreat.

Spoiler: He's not flexible.

He steps onto the stone, squints at pigeons like they owe him money.

Then stops. Five metres away.

He doesn't know which brown face is his problem. Beautiful.

· · ·

He clears his throat. Like this is a meeting.

Like I'll pop up with a clipboard and say, "Welcome to your redemption arc."

He places the bag gently at the base of a tourist sculpture. Like an offering to a god he doesn't believe in.

Then turns, slow, performative, and walks.

I count: One, two, three...

No spin. No second glance.

He's scared, but trained - predator habits die with the next invoice, not before.

I wait. Ten minutes. Enough time for karma to take a selfie.

Then I walk up, lift the bag, and keep moving.

1:22 p.m. – Yarra Footbridge

Unzipped in the shadow of a half-dead gum tree.

Bricks. Neat. Banded. Clean like conscience rarely is.

$50,000 AUD.

Twenty-five girls' tuition fees. Or one man's silence.

Phone buzzes.

Rekha: *Coffee after class? Feel better today.*

Me: *Running an errand. See you tonight. Keep the day bright.*

Send.

I watch a tram slide past Federation Square like nothing ever happened.

Because nothing ever does - not publicly.

Ledger Update:

• A\$ 50,000 silence

• One predator now scanning exit signs

• No apologies. No headlines. No closure.

• One story rewritten - but only in private.

Do I feel better?

No.

But I feel level.

And for people like me, *level* is the closest thing we get to witness protection.

What's justice if you can't hold it without washing your hands?

22 ZEROED BALANCE

The morning after the hand-off, I walked the length of Elizabeth Street with Dev's duffel strapped to my back like a recycled sin.

Three forex shops blinked neon promises: BEST RATE · NO QUESTIONS · GST INCLUDED. I chose the one without a camera. The woman behind the bulletproof glass looked like she'd processed war crimes before lunch.

I split the money like a surgeon handling conjoined nerves.

→ AU$ 29,500 to *Amma's* SBI savings.

→ AU$ 20,500 to *Achan's* current.

Both transfers end in 500. That way, it looks like tuition, not hush money. Even guilt needs rounding.

The teller asked if I needed a receipt.

"Yes, please. Two copies. Frame-worthy."

Outside, on the footpath, I deleted all GPS metadata.

Encrypted the videos. Uploaded them to a server hosted somewhere between Iceland and revenge. Then I emailed *Amma* and *Achan*:

• MEDICAL FEES

• RENT BRIDGE

Subjects that sound serious, but say nothing.

Late afternoon in Kottayam, they crossed the street to Roy's storefront - receipts warm in their hands.

But the shutters were down.

The Laxmi Financials sign had vanished, like a promise past its warranty.

The neighbour pharmacist shrugged: "He flew to Dubai this morning. Family emergency."

• • •

Yes. The emergency's name was *me*.

The deeds? Gone.

The files? Gone.

Roy? Gone, but still breathing somewhere tax-neutral.

Back in Thomastown, the tube light buzzed like a witness with a conscience.

My phone buzzed louder.

Voice note. Unknown number.

I hit play.

"Smart boy. Killing the golden cow."

"But city is small. Debts grow back."

No name. No signature. But I didn't need either.

Roy's voice always smelled faintly of Old Spice and exit fees.

The ledger, when I finally wrote it out, looked neat. Too neat.

.   .   .

Description Status

Principal (₹600,000) Paid

Interest (₹36,000) Paid

Collateral (chain, bangles) Returned or pawned

Roy's leverage ???

I backed up the files. Shredded the originals.

Then took out *Amma*'s thin gold chain, looped it around my neck - not as jewellery, but as proof we made it out with at least *one* thing intact.

Outside, the gutters shook from wind.

Inside, for the first time in 118 days, I couldn't hear the clock.

But I didn't call it peace.

Peace is what you feel when there's no one left to answer to.

This? This was just a pause.

Roy may be gone.

But men like Roy are never really off the clock.

They're just adjusting the interest rate.

· · ·

Ledger Note (Postscript):

- Principal cleared

- Threat relocated

- One golden cow escaped the slaughter, for now

23 HANDLE BAR HEAT

After the last transfer cleared and Roy's texts turned to silence, I told myself I was out.

Debt repaid. Ledger zeroed. Ghost exorcised.

Trang didn't get the memo.

———

I was eating leftover rice in the Cactus Court kitchen when he messaged:

TRANG: One last run? Light. Easy.

Just a favour, bro. Not even that far.

No one else I trust.

Trust. That word again.

I ignored it.

He called.

"One drop, Arjun. I'm drowning. Do it for me, not the game."

I owed him.

Trang's runs were how I got Roy off my neck, how I paid back the ghosts and bought silence with interest.

So I said yes - **once**.

The next morning, Trang was already waiting outside.

Grey hoodie, cigarette tucked behind his ear like punctuation.

He handed me a small envelope and a backpack.

.   .   .

"Envelope to Docklands. Bag to Sunshine."

I gave him a look.

"You said one drop."

He grinned.

"Two-for-one special. Promise - nothing shady. Just trust the zip."

Sunshine drop was quick. Park bench. No eye contact. The kind of silence you don't interrupt.

On the ride back, I stopped at a servo for water.

Outside, a kid in a knockoff Deliveroo jacket was getting yelled at.

Not just yelled - **cornered** by two men and a red Corolla.

Trang's people.

I didn't intervene.

Didn't breathe until I crossed the bridge near Docklands.

The next time Trang called, I didn't answer.

He called again. And again.

Then he showed up outside my lecture hall, leaning against the bike racks like he belonged there.

"You're in this, bro. You know the cycle. You ride, you eat. You stop riding-"

He tapped his temple.

"People forget they owe you grace."

I told him I was done.

He just laughed, handed me another envelope.

"Long as you stay loyal, nothing touches you. You know that."

I took it.

Because it's easier to ride than argue.

Because part of me still thought the chain between Trang and me was thinner than the one Roy once looped around my family.

Because in this city, every freedom feels like a courier run: fast, silent, and one stop away from regret.

24 VISITOR HOURS

Thomastown, Friday, 10 November 2017

11:18 p.m.

Thomastown station coughs us out like even the possums called it a night.

Rekha's holding a bag of staff-expired croissants. I carry chicken skin in a freezer pouch, burn on my arm still hissing. Neon buzzes down Main Street like it wants a refund. Then I see the house:

All lights on.

Never a good sign.

———

The kitchen's already in full courtroom mode.

. . .

Grey blazer, suitcase still tagged MEL ⇄ SYD. Mouth pacing faster than feet.

"Zainab, apa ni? Your parents trust me. I come, I see this?"

Zainab leans on the fridge. Hijab skewed, face bracing.

Kartik barefoot, CFA notes hugged like a flotation device.

Uncle Jamal. Confirmed.

He switches to machine-gun Malay-English:

"They send you here for study, not romance-romance! And this fella-this boy-hold your hand like pasar malam discount!"

Kartik gets called "boy." First time I see him without a rebuttal.

I don't even like Kartik. But this isn't about liking.

It's about recognising a pattern, and deciding I won't be the silence that lets it finish.

Maybe that's what survival means now: not just escaping the fire, but pulling others out-even if I'm still burning.

. . .

Rekha steps forward, calm but loaded.

"Sir, I'm Rekha. Nepal, not on your payroll. Zainab and Kartik are adults. Rent paid. CGPA stable. No scandal. No problem."

Jamal eyes her like she's an unlicensed taxi.

"I not need lecture, okay? Her father say, I take care. But now Instagram show you two, like Bollywood love story. Very dramatic!"

Kartik tries diplomacy: "Uncle, my intention-"

"Intention? Intention can buy Maggi noodles or not?" Jamal snaps.

Rekha doesn't blink. "He studies finance. At least he can calculate your opinion's interest rate."

Kartik nearly laughs. Jamal doesn't.

I step beside Rekha. Quiet. Sharp.

.   .   .

"We live five in one shoebox. We know who reset Wi-Fi at 3 a.m., who washes dishes, who kicks Zainab up for Fajr after her double shift. That's Kartik. He carries weight. Do you?"

The house holds its breath. Even Sanjay pauses in the hallway.

Jamal's blazer slips an inch off his shoulder.

"Okay. Okay. Study first, then maybe talk. Understand?"

Zainab nods. It's not surrender. It's containment.

Jamal jabs a finger. "Tomorrow morning. Preston Motel. I call her father. You"-at Kartik-"bring your intention."

Suitcase wheels scrape across the tiles. Door clicks shut. Too quiet. Worse than a slam.

———

The fridge starts humming again, like a generator checking the damage.

.   .   .

Zainab restacks the plates like it's the only thing she can still control.

Kartik stares at the linoleum like he's lost the formula.

Rekha whispers, "Tea?" No one moves. Steam doesn't lie. It floats around us, heavy with everything we didn't say.

I drop the chicken skin into the freezer.

Outside: silence. Inside: rage curling up, waiting.

Think of Dev in Sydney. Roy's ticking clock. Uncles like Jamal, entitled and unchecked.

Melbourne's real syllabus? Survival Science 101.

Keep every receipt. Especially the human kind.

Phone buzzes. Roy again:

"Debt clear, da. But business not finish. One day, you pay exit fee. I'll call when clock says."

The numbers may read zero, but Roy always counts in shadows.

Somewhere between Roy's file and Dev's grin, I stopped believing in clean exits.

But this-this felt almost right.

Not justice. But friction. Enough to slow a man like Jamal down.

I file the message where threats go. Then set the alarm.

07:00 a.m.

Not for class.

For whatever 'exit fee' turns out to be.

25 UNLABELLED BOTTLES

The week after Uncle Jamal's ambush felt like life inside a battery cage- no fresh wounds, just feathers drifting everywhere.

Sanjay locked himself in his room. At odd hours, we caught Gujarati whispers through the wall: *Maa... ghar... thaki gayo chu.* On Thursday, a Jetstar e-ticket to Ahmedabad appeared under a fridge magnet, cooling its regret.

Zainab floated through the kitchen like a shadow that tidies. She thanked Rekha with silent bowls of dal and never met Kartik's eyes.

. . .

Kartik ghosted between CFA podcasts and half-written apologies. Every ringtone made him flinch, certain Jamal sat on the other end.

———

Friday, 6:40 p.m. Rekha and I were rating instant noodles (edible if desperate) when Zainab knocked cheeks pink from a double shift.

"I owe you both," she said, voice small but steady. "Day trip tomorrow- vineyard in Yarra. I'll pay petrol."

Kartik materialised behind her, hands pocketed. "I'll drive," he offered, half-dare, half-penance.

We asked Sanjay, but his door answered with silence. The Ahmedabad ticket was louder.

Departure locked: 7:00 a.m., rental Corolla, four shaky passengers.

———

Fog still hugged Darebin Creek when we rolled out. Kartik's knuckles were white on the wheel; motivational Punjabi spat from Spotify, then skipped.

· · ·

Rekha and I shared the back seat with a box of bakery croissants, portable amnesty.

Halfway to Yarra Glen a message pinged the group chat: *Boarding. Sorry. Need home food + reset.-* Sanjay, already at the gate. Blue ticks, no replies. Even the speaker quit humming.

———

MüllrHaus Vines-name ' name is full of umlauts, none of us could pronounce. Vines marched downhill; a Labrador greeted us like rehearsed hospitality.

Florence poured free tastings. Zainab raised her glass: "To debt-less fun." The smile landed maybe seventy per cent. Rekha spat every sample; the 3 a.m. bakery shift loomed. I drank hers too; warmth pooled fast.

Dusk bonfire: pallets crackled, bottles circled, questions suspended. Zainab's laugh finally found fifth gear; Kartik tried a barrel joke, then drifted to the fence, phone glowing.

Rekha leaned into my shoulder. "Feels borrowed, doesn't it?"

"Expensive rental," I said. She told me her grandfather judged evenings by courtyard silence; this hush, she said, tasted rented, not owned. We watched embers fall until Kartik's voice cracked behind us-"Maybe Brisbane... maybe home."

———

2:10 a.m., Thomastown. The house looked asleep but tense, like a dog pretending not to guard. Zainab pressed the last croissant into Rekha's hand: "You keep proving strangers can be next of kin." Rekha only shrugged.

Kartik packed in the dark; by 4:00 a.m., an Uber swallowed his suitcase. He muttered goodbye to no one, destination "a mate's couch, just for a bit."

Zainab at the doorway, arms folded. "At least he chose something," she said when the tail-lights turned the corner.

Kitchen light buzzed. Rekha poured water; her fingers brushed mine, deliberate. "Two down," she whispered. I nodded, unsure whether the house was safer or emptier.

———

Phone buzzed-**Roy**:

"Debt clear, da, but don't start holiday.

Business not over.

I come to collect 'exit fee' face-to-face soon."

. . .

Menace, succinct.

I achieved the threat, but my thumb hesitated half a beat, long enough to admit worry still fits inside a paid-off ledger.

Another ping- University Compliance: *Attendance breach, visa 8202 under review. Contact us within five business days.*

So one predator leaves, another clock starts.

Rekha set her glass down, eyes searching my face. I kissed her forehead instead of confessing: night rides, Dev's money, Roy's exit fee receipts, I keep in silence.

Tomorrow we'll need new rosters, new rent math, fresh lies to fill the vacancies. Tonight we stand in fluorescent quiet, tasting unlabelled wine and wondering how many departures a share-house can survive before the walls apply for permanent residency.

26 COLLECTORS AT THE DOOR

There are knocks you hear. And knocks that remember where you live.

The knock came just after midnight - four raps. Quick-quick-pause.

The rhythm of someone who'd practised it. On doors like mine. In suburbs like this.

Rekha was already gone to bakery shift.

Zainab snored behind two locked doors.

Sanjay's monitor glowed League of Legends blue.

I cracked the front door.

. . .

Two Malayalee boys stood dripping on the concrete.

Uni hoodies. Delivery helmets. Nerves showing at the cuffs.

The shorter one handed me a flyer - Laxmi Financials, rain-warped.

One Sharpie line across the top:

EXIT FEE – SETTLE FACE TO FACE.

Of course.

Tall one: "Need talk, chetta."

His accent was Thrissur meets bravado.

"Roy say principal cleared. But exit still pending."

Me: "How much is 'exit'?"

They exchanged glances - even collectors didn't get the decimal point.

Short one: "Roy decide later. We collect promise tonight."

. . .

I stepped onto the porch, body blocking the doorway like it owed me rent.

Me: "Let me guess-you owe him too?"

That pierced the uniform. Their spines dropped half an inch.

Debt knows its own cousins.

Tall one tried: "He helps us study. Now we help him settle. One round."

One round. Like it was a board game. Like we weren't all one bad day away from pawning our own futures.

The porch light caught the burn scar on my forearm - mango acid, orchard gift.

The oil stain on my jeans.

The chain around my neck.

Me: "Tell Roy next time he visits, he better wear body armour. The clock's still ticking - but now it's ticking for him."

. . .

Short one looked at my eyes like he'd never met someone who'd closed a ledger and survived.

The old one stepped forward. Late 30s. Knees worn from security gigs.

He reached inside his jacket. Slowly. Like drawing a weapon or a memory.

Pulled out a thumb drive. Scuffed. Blue plastic. Like a kindergarten pen drive, if kindergartens dealt in blackmail.

Him: "He asked me to fix a laptop. Back in Kottayam. Said it was overheating. I copied all files to a thumb drive to back it up. Meant to delete. Never did."

His hand shook, but not from fear — from remembering which parts he never agreed to witness.

A pause. His eyes not meeting mine.

Him: "Insurance, you know. For days like this."

He looked older than his face. The kind of tired that comes from watching too many men make promises that float.

. . .

Then, softer:

"You know he started honest, right? Roy?"

"He used to help people. When the first boy from our junction got into UK universities - Roy found a way to raise the deposit. After that... more came. And more. Then he started charging. Then promising. Then printing. Every story needed a shortcut."

A breath. Then:

"You do favours too long... you forget what help is. All he remembers now is leverage."

I took the drive. Turned it over. No label. No password. No protection.

Inside it would be:

• Visa scans.

• Guarantor deeds.

• Interest statements, fake and real.

• The roster of Roy's little empire - Cairns to Kalgoorlie.

All names. All desperate.

I saw my own name flash in the back of my head like a guilty hologram.

I copied the drive to cloud.

Backed it up again on a burner account.

Then slipped the USB into the toe of an unused sock.

The flyer? I flushed it. That paper doesn't deserve recycling.

On the porch, I folded a new flyer - blank this time - into a paper plane and handed it back to them.

Me: "Tonight you walk away empty. Next time, walk away lighter."

The porch light buzzed overhead. The fridge compressor thumped once, like a laugh with asthma.

The younger boys backed off down the steps.

"We come back," Tall called over his shoulder -

It sounded more like a prayer than a threat.

. . .

I didn't reply.

I watched their tail-lights wobble off like feathers from Roy's dying bird.

Latch clicked. House exhaled.

Debt changes shape. Sometimes it shows up with your father's name on the envelope.

Roy thinks the story's over.

What he doesn't know is that some files don't just save - they replicate.

27 CONFESSIONS

Thomastown, Thursday, 21 December 2017

Phone lights up.

Headline:

"POLICE SHUT DOWN MELBOURNE BIKE-DRUG SYNDICATE — FIVE ARRESTS, COURIERS SOUGHT."

Photo's grainy, but I know that helmet. That posture. That front wheel turned slightly outward.

Telegram pings.

Trang: "Need rider tonight, one gap, A$ 400. Quick yes?"

. . .

I type *can't*.

Delete.

Thumb hovers.

7:43 a.m. - Laundry Shed

Rekha's already outside, squatting on the concrete. Hoodie up. Eyes down.

The wet floor shines around her like a border.

I pause. Say nothing.

She speaks first.

"Looked familiar. That helmet."

She doesn't raise her voice. Doesn't need to.

Tone like a locked drawer - you know there's weight inside.

I say, "It's over."

Rekha nods once. "I don't get the feeling that it is."

. . .

Then silence again.

Steam rises from the laundry vent behind us like guilt with nowhere to settle.

14 Dec · 10:12 p.m. - Lounge

TV mutters a cricket replay. No one's watching.

Telegram buzzes.

Trang: "Police quiet now, bro. One small drop- pay good money, can?"

I accept.

Reflex, not decision.

Rekha walks out of the bathroom, toweling her hair.

She catches the tail end of the message and the gloves in my lap.

Her eyes don't narrow. That would mean surprise.

She just takes one second too long to blink.

·   ·   ·

Pause.

Then:

"You're still delivering?"

I lie with the speed of someone who's lied before.

"Just this once."

She walks past me without another word.

No fight. No cry.

Just the sound of trust shifting its weight.

15 Dec · 7:40 p.m. - Back Patio

Steam curls from our noodle bowls. We haven't eaten. We won't.

She breaks the silence.

"You kept all of it under the doona. The deliveries. The money. The risk. Me - under the same roof - and I had no idea."

I stare into the bowl like it might explain me.

. . .

She shakes her head.

"I don't need a saviour, Arjun. I needed a partner."

I try: "I thought I was protecting you."

She laughs. Small, bitter.

"That's what Dev said."

She stands. No shouting. Just silence so full of judgment it creaks.

3 Jan · 9:11 a.m. - University Email

Subject: **Attendance Breach – Visa 8202 Review**

"Please attend International Compliance, 10 Jan, 10:00 a.m."

Melbourne: where even probation is issued in Times New Roman.

The email came with no greeting, no sign-off. Just digital breathlessness and a ticking clock.

I clicked 'Mark as Unread' — as if that might reset the countdown.

. . .

6 Jan · 6:50 p.m. - Front Porch

Another knock.

This one's taller. Shoulders like bricks. Nothing student about him.

"Roy wants his exit fee timetable."

I almost laugh. Roy's gone - Dubai, probably.

But ghosts have reliable couriers.

"Interest ended," I say.

"Exit's different," he says.

Same words. New tone.

He hands me nothing. Just a look like I'll see him again.

9 Jan · 11:10 p.m. - Bedroom

Rekha's apron still smells like bakery grease and courage.

. . .

She's scrolling something, but not really reading.

"Visa meeting tomorrow?"

I nod.

She doesn't ask what I'll say.

Then, softly:

"Anything else I should know before it knocks me over in the kitchen again?"

I slide the phone over.

She scrolls:

Maps. Payments. Photos.

The courier routes. The cash log. The warning texts.

She reads slowly. Not because it's complex, but because it confirms what she already suspected.

. . .

She hands it back.

"You survived," she says.

Then:

"So did I. Alone. I won't do alone again."

Pause.

"Next semester, we survive together. Or we don't bother."

10 Jan · 10:00 a.m. - International Compliance

Fluorescent lighting. Pleasantly neutral interrogation.

I say what I have to:

"Yes, I was unwell."

"Yes, I've recommitted to my course."

"Yes, I have a new timetable."

Warning issued. Not cancellation.

Melbourne forgives - in writing only.

·   ·   ·

10 Jan · 8:47 p.m. - Our Room

Rekha's beside me, reading the bakery roster.

We don't speak much.

Then she puts the list down.

"We can't keep lying and calling it strategy."

I nod. That's all I can offer.

But this time, I mean it.

The silence between us isn't empty this time — it's working.

We're not fixing anything, but we've stopped making it worse.

Updated Scorecard:

• Visa: Probation

• Rekha: Still here

• Roy: Replaced by someone with broader shoulders

• Trust: On instalments

• Truth: No longer optional

· · ·

10 Jan · 9:41 p.m. — Front Door

Another knock.

This one is polite.

Even before I open it, I feel the difference - not Roy's ghost, not Trang's shadow.

Two officers. One male, one female. Both in plain clothes.

Badges. Not flashing. Just presented - like proof of weather changing.

"Mr. Arjun Nair?"

I nod.

"We're following up on a courier investigation. You're not under arrest. But we'd like you to come to Northcote Police Station tomorrow, 11:00 a.m. Just a few questions."

They hand me a card. White. Boring. Official.

· · ·

"You've seen the news. We're asking everyone who might've worked for a company called Trang Logistics."

I nod again. Don't trust my voice.

They leave with nods like neighbours, not cops.
I close the door gently.

Rekha looks up from her tea.

"What now?"

I stare at the card.

No answer yet. Just a time, a place, and a city that keeps remembering what you hoped would be forgotten.

28 BETWEEN BADGE AND BLADE

Northcote Police Station, Friday, 12 January 2018

Pastel walls, Australian Coat of Arms, yesterday's *Herald Sun*. I rehearse my name twice under my breath.

————

10:03 a.m. - Interview Room 2

Detective Sergeant Price skims the file.

"*Ar-jurn* Nair, right?"

"Ar-jun," I correct. Short *u*, rhymes with **run**.

He doesn't adjust.

. . .

Folder flips open-grainy CCTV of me rolling a blue Giant out of Footscray at 1:06 p.m.

"This you, *Ar-jurn?*"

"Yes." Voice steady.

"And the man you ride for Trang? How cosy are you two?" He says Trang the way people say *tarantula*.

"Not cosy. We share a mutual friend- Wei."

Price leans back, laces fingers over stomach like a judge who's already bored of guilt.

"Funny, Wei never shows on Trang's phone logs. Been listening since November- lot of chatter, none of it kosher. You want to tell me why your name pops where his pings?"

"Wrong place, wrong shift."

"That line's popular this season." He taps the photo of the bike. "Good students keep hobbies like chess."

Good students, sure. We study, mop kitchens, vanish on graduation day- quiet credits rolling under fluorescent detention lights. Plenty of brown faces land in lock-ups; the glossy visa brochure just air-brushes them out.

I hold the stare. "I'm here to cooperate. What exactly do you need?"

He slides a card across. "If Trang calls, you call me before, not after. Helpful witnesses earn breathing room, Mr Nair."

Finally, he gets the name right; damage already done.

I pocket the card like it might rot through my jeans, smile just enough to pass for grateful, and file his tone under debts I'll repay in silence.

———

12 Jan · 7:32 p.m. - Outside Cactus Court, drizzle

Phone buzzes. **Trang**.

"Courier boy, heard you spent quality time with cops." His laugh is all molars.

"Routine questions."

"Routine ruins businesses. One more run fixes everything. Warehouse Westmeadows, Saturday. Boss man wants to eyeball you."

"I'm out."

"You don't quit; you expire. Show up, 22:00. Bring the blue bike- you know your place."

Line dies. Rain keeps tapping the screen like a second warning.

———

13 Jan · 10:04 p.m. - Back alley, under faulty lamp

Text from Trang:

"Remember, courier: no show, no future. "

Knife-clock emoji. Simple algebra.

Price's card in my left pocket; Trang's threat in my right; Rekha's flyer between them like a fragment of clean air.

Three doors, one body. Decision pending.

———

13 Jan · 8:12 p.m. - Shared Room

Rekha drops a glossy flyer on the duvet: **"Seasonal Orchard Jobs · Kununurra · Free Hostel"**

Dada's WhatsApp avatar grins from the corner.

"I withdrew this morning. No more tuition-in-circles. Fresh reset up north."

My throat sticks. "You quit the course?"

"Better than quitting myself." She folds the flyer, looks straight through me. "You could come-escape clocks, debts, exits."

I can't say the warehouse name, the partner request, the exit fee. I just nod once- pending.

She packs uniforms into a Woolworths tote. Croissant crumbs on the mattress feel like evidence.

———

13 Jan · 10:04 p.m. - Laneway Behind Woolworths

Text from Trang:

"GPS drop set. If you ghost, we both haunt-understood? "

Knife emoji again, clock emoji, simple algebra.

· · ·

I pocket the phone, feel Price's card in the same jeans, and hear Rekha's orchard wind rustling somewhere far north.

Three vectors: Police, warehouse, Kimberley sky.

Whichever line I follow, somebody's waiting.

29 DEADLINE FOR DEPARTURE

University Office, Tuesday, 16 January 2018

"Mr ... Nyer?"

"Nair. *Ar-jun Nair.*"

Officer Pappas- Heritage-Week bunting, laser stare-scrolls, frowns.

"Zero lectures since Week 4."

"I've been attending reality-shift work, couch-surf roulette, phantom placements. Your brochure skipped those electives."

"Visa 8202: enrol, attend."

"I'm busy breathing. The 'Melbourne Dream' invoices by the hour."

. . .

She exhales. "Solution?"

"One-semester deferral. Family crisis. I'll restart mid-year with cash and lungs."

"Need medical or compassionate proof."

"Compassionate: dad's pharmacy is drowning in loan-shark interest."

I slide a Malayalam pawn slip and a bleeding cash-flow sheet.

She nods. "Deposit still due-$7,900, non-refundable."

"Paid today."

APPROVED - PENDING PAYMENT thumps the carbon.

"Lose this and the system eats you."

"Already nibbling."

She finally nails my name: "Good luck, Mr Nair."

Outside, the sun feels prepaid- expires on the next swipe. I file the yellow slip beside my passport and draft an exit north.

————

17 Jan · 1:43 p.m. - Food-court Wi-Fi

Visa deferred. Police and Trang orbit.

A seven-day window before the next audit.

Tickets

• Jetstar MEL → Darwin · 25 Jan 06:45 · A$ 189 · carry-on only

• Greyhound Darwin → Kununurra · 25 Jan 20:00 · A$ 85 · overnight

Dev's hush money covers the escape budget.

Rekha texts: *Roster cleared. North it is.* One green tick-no emoji. Forgiveness still in draft.

————

18 Jan · 9:20 p.m. - Room 3B

Carry-on: 7 kg max.

Keep: two uniforms, three tees, SD card, charger-cam, *Amma's* chain, Rekha's anklet, passports, deferral slip.

Dump: Kochi-humidity suitcase, phantom lecture notes, grease-stained shirts. Deleting browser tabs of my old life.

———

19 Jan · 8:55 a.m. - Post Office

Padded envelope to Detective Price: GPS file, Trang's knife-clock text. No return address.

Note: "Loose end, not confession." Tracking slip, keep-trust needs receipts.

———

22 Jan · 10:04 p.m. - Lounge

News crawl: Footscray ring "under inquiry." Faces still pixelated.

Phone pings:

Trang: *Warehouse silent. Don't torch bridges you'll need.*

Price: *Any update? Help us help you.*

Unread = armour.

———

24 Jan · 11:58 p.m. - SkyBus Rank

Rekha hands Zainab the key and six croissants.

"Lease ends next month. If the walls ask, say we went north."

Our packs rattle- past lighter, guilt louder.

———

25 Jan · 4:35 a.m. - Tullamarine T4

Boarding passes spit. Phone flares:

Trang: *Top End's still Australia, brother. Clocks reach everywhere.*

Price: *Call before deeper trouble.*

Two ghosts on the manifest.

Security weighs us: 6.8 kg each.

Gate lounge. Rekha leans in.

"Middle of nowhere," she murmurs.

"Middle of something else," I say.

· · ·

"Boarding Darwin service JQ 647."

We rise. Melbourne drifts off-screen like an unpaid invoice. In my pocket, two numbers blink-detective, dealer- waiting for Kununurra to decide which alarm rings first.

FILE THREE
പഴം · PAZHAM
FRUIT

*Kununurra: mango rows that peel skin, weld blisters, and
teach me how cheap a body rents for.*

30 RUNWAYS & ROADWAYS

9:10 a.m. – Melbourne slips under the wing. Row 27 still exhales leftover city air-wet wool, instant coffee, commuter fatigue caught in the vents. The wing slices a white corridor through cloud; it feels like ripping the "ABSENT" stamp out of my future.

———

Darwin stopover, 3:20 p.m.

Heat blasts up the jet-bridge; arrivals hall smells of bleach, fryer oil, tired jet fuel. Rekha's glasses fog- muscle memory from nursing labs she has now ghosted. One A$ 4.60 iced coffee dies in two gulps.

· · ·

"Tastes like failing anatomy," she says, draining the last of the iced coffee. "My COE's in palliative care - that's the Confirmation of Enrolment, the single sheet that keeps a student visa heart beating."

I almost reply *debt never dies*, decide silence weighs less in carry-on.

———

Night bus, Stuart Highway

Engine hum shivers through the floor; termite mounds ghost by in moonlight-cathedrals built by insects that never clock off. Rekha shifts, ankle puffed from hauling the duffel stamped **FRAGILE / HOPE**. Water sips become rationed coins.

Adelaide River roadhouse sells *ROAD-KILL PIE* and crimson-seasoned fries.

"We might survive," I say.

"Define survive," she answers, tightening her lace. The bruise is a dull plum-background ache, not yet plot-hinge.

Back on board, her breathing anchors on my shoulder- first time her sleep trusts my skeleton outside Melbourne postcode.

Katherine Servo, 2:00 a.m.

Mounted TV loops cyclone warnings: *Marcus may re-intensify toward Kimberley mid-March.*

I picture mango branches snapping, sap glittering like glass. Rekha half-dreams in Nepali: *Ama, mat jayo- don't leave, Mother.* The plea dissolves into the night.

Dawn over the Ord

Greyhound #821 exhales beside a fridge-sized sign:

KUNUNURRA 5 308 - a town small enough to remember every stranger's mistake.

The bus rolls south; timetable becomes dust.

Iron-oxide grit tastes like tea boiled thrice on a kerosene stove. Heat rises off bitumen; air drags through my throat like corduroy.

Outside the servo, a sun-bleached poster flaps: **Ord Valley Muster • May 11-20** - proof the town plans to outlive storms and fruit pickers alike.

. . .

Rekha swings the heavier pack without comment. I spit red dust and realise the rasp in my chest is Melbourne vowels still squatting rent-free. I cough them into Kimberley heat and wonder, without lecture codes, with one bruised ankle and a half-charged phone, what language we'll learn to breathe next.

31 ARRIVAL AT KUN-UN-URRA

Kununurra, Saturday, 3 March 2018

The long-haul bus sighed us onto pavement the colour of rusted coins. *Kununurra-kun-un-urra,* the driver grunted-four syllables that tasted like dry toast-then his tail-lights vanished into Kimberley dark.

A lone sodium lamp buzzed above the depot, dragging every moth in the postcode into its orbit. Rekha and I stood beneath it, bags at our feet, feeling more like soft fruit dropped at the wrong loading dock than travellers with a plan. Heat was already seeping from the tarmac; my phone flashed **92 % humidity** once, then fainted.

Two Aboriginal kids cruised past on BMXs, half-awake. One gave me the quickest nod-almost conspiratorial, a blink-long recognition that none of us matched the brochure. I nodded back; treaty signed. A ute rattles past- driver's stare Velcro hooks to two brown faces on his moving menu. A second ute coasted slower, its passenger craning for a longer look.

"They think I'm Chinese," Rekha muttered.

"Or lost cargo," I said. Humour: cheapest armour we own.

Backpacks knocking hips, we hunted phone reception the way desert people hunt soak water. The town shrank to a one-kilometre ribbon-servo, IGA, bait-and-tackle, shire office shuttered against cyclone gossip. Above, the sky rusted from slate to pink.

Neon at **Kunnaburger-Home of the Kimberley Heart-Starter** promised ALL-DAY BREAKFAST; door chained. Next-door laundromat boasted ICE COLD DRINKS + FREE Wi-Fi, as if bytes and refrigeration were cousins. Rekha pressed her phone to the glass: one bar, gone.

"Carrier pigeons would unionise here," she sighed.

"Plenty of work, no award wage," I said.

Past a mural of boabs dancing under stars, an older Miriwoong man in hi-vis lifted two fingers. I lifted three. Negotiations concluded.

·   ·   ·

The Savannah Sun Motel blinked VACANCY like an indecisive firefly. The receptionist-polo shirt faded by wet seasons- held our faces a beat too long before sliding a key across laminate. "Room twelve. Swampy cooler conks out after lunch- give her a whack."

Inside: ceiling-fan rattling like loose prayer beads, kettle determined to burn remorse out of instant coffee. I fired off one line to *Amma-Reached WA safe, starting internship tomorrow. All good.* Phone back-off; lies pack lighter than explanations.

We dialled the orchard hotline plastered on Dada's flyer. Straight to voicemail. I imagined him steering a ute into No-Service country, Nokia tossed among mango crates.

"Maybe WA Fridays knock off early," I said.

"Undertakers knock off early," Rekha replied. "Corpses keep arriving."

At Mirima-mini Bungle Bungles of rusted sandstone, we shared Woollies peanuts under a bloodwood, sketching a coastal café on the back of the receipt: her pastries, my "apps." "*Appam?*" she teased; sweat blurred our laughter. On the walk back she rolled her ankle, just a hiss of breath-bruise, not plot twist, yet.

·　·　·

The motel air-con surrendered before sunset. We lay under the fan, urgency spliced with quiet. When she slept, an unknown number buzzed once, no message. Whatever debt rode north with us was still breathing.

Before dawn, the phone vibrated again: unknown. *"Arjun? Coles car park. Seven sharp. Bring paperwork."* Click. At least he used my name.

Rekha laced swollen boots, eyebrow raised in silent diagnosis. We stepped into air so hot it felt pre-chewed. Behind us, the VACANCY sign blinked to nobody; ahead, the highway shimmered like a mirage pretending to be water. In my pocket: one boarding-pass stub, a fake internship, and a voicemail we couldn't replay. Whatever language the Kimberley spoke, it was about to test our accent.

32 BURLEY MAN, BITTER FRUIT

Kununurra, Monday, 5 March 2018

Coles car park   6:58 a.m.

If purgatory had asphalt it would look like the Coles lot at dawn-trolleys rattling, ibis poking chip packets for prophecy. Rekha and I stood with our packs like two items left off a grocery list. A white HiLux growled in.

"Ar-june?" The driver bit off the name as if the month owed him rent.

"Tools in back." No greeting, no paperwork.

Rekha winced, climbing into the tray; I wedged between two plastic drums that smelled of fertiliser and roadkill. The cab glass sealed any attempt at conversation.

. . .

Bitumen gave way to red dirt, every corrugation punching guilt up my spine. Mango grids unrolled to every horizon, green quilts sewn for foreign shelves.

Office demountable   8:12 a.m.

Prefab office, blistered paint, generator coughing. Out lumbered a barrel-chested man stitched together from pub fights: buzz-cut, sun-scalded biceps, faded anchors on skin.

"Andrew D'Rosario," he said. "People call me Dada." The nickname came out like a debt.

He flipped through our passports, paused a beat too long on Rekha's photo.

"Students, huh? Soft hands. Quotas'll hurt." Passports landed on a filing cabinet like expired coupons.

Soft hands, I thought- another label to file beside Roy's "exit fee," Dev's "good girl," Trang's "courier bro." New town, same drawer of men who measure you by what they can squeeze out.

"Cabin 7. Rules on the door. Miss breakfast, your problem. Miss quota-mine." He vanished into the tin gloom; country music started up, cheerful and merciless.

Cabin 7   8:40 a.m.

Shipping containers pretending to be housing: one window, two bunks. Fan rattled like loose prayer beads; taps spat rust.

Rekha rolled her ankle gently. "Tender, not broken."

"Tell it medical cover costs extra," I offered; levity clanged. Outside, mango trees waited in parade formation, fruit still green but gossiping about ripening.

Canteen   6:09 a.m.

Thirty pickers hunched over plastic tables: sun-bleached locals, sand-dusted backpackers, a shy knot of Indonesians. Joseph, the cook, with a Manila accent, Midland detour, ladled curry. "Used to sauté scallops," he grinned. "Now I boil things till they apologise."

Janice, ex-flight attendant from Penang, pushed a plate our way. "Eat double; tomorrow you'll burn it by breakfast."

Stories surfaced: visas priced like weddings, résumés gone feral, towns that run on rumours.

Dada lounged at the doorway, arms folded, gaze stuck to Rekha-linger, shift, linger. My spoon slipped; he smirked and melted into dark, silent as a croc into billabong water.

Night cracks open

Lights out; geckos clicked along the wall like faulty clocks. Rekha rubbed tiger balm into her ankle, jaw set.

Next door, backpackers argued crate bonuses: "Eighty bucks if you hit eighteen, mate-before tax!"

.   .   .

Dada's ute coughed somewhere beyond the cabins, laughter sharp as wire.

I texted *Amma* a single line: *All fine. Internship west going well. Talk soon.* Lies fold smaller than truth in a 4 G blackout. Phone dipped to one bar, then none.

Outside, petrol generators droned lullabies in the key of fatigue. A night bird sobbed-three notes up, one sliding down, practising regret. Rekha's breathing slowed; I matched it, counting heartbeats against corrugated tin, wondering which would dent first: mango crates, borrowed promises, or the steel inside a man who calls himself Dada and fixes problems "quick."

33 QUOTA BAPTISM

Ord Valley Orchard, Tuesday, 6 March 2018

5:47 a.m.

Mango mornings don't rise - they erupt.

One minute it's twilight, the next, the sun's throwing punches.

We - backpackers, boat people, degree refugees - stand like discounted produce waiting for markdown.

Dada's HiLux backfires into existence, smoke curling behind it like a grudge.

He steps out with a stubby in hand, stopwatch clipped to his belt like holy scripture.

. . .

Burra trails him - ex-roo shooter, now Field Supervisor. Six-foot-forever. Clipboard in one hand, picking bags in the other. Talks in verbs: *lift*, *move*, *shut*. Nouns are a luxury.

Burra doesn't dock wages. He "respects gravity."

———

The whiteboard glares at us.

ARJUN A. NAIR: 22?

REKHA THAPA: 20 (inj.)

RAHIM FAMILY: 22 each

That question mark after my name weighs more than any crate.

"Soft hands never make sunset," Dada says.

He tosses me a bag. Latex dust puffs. I breathe it in.

———

First row: green fruit.

Snip - sap hits my wrist.

Second snip - skin itches.

Third - blister.

By the fourth, I stop counting. Numbers can't afford therapy.

Rekha's beside me, ankle strapped, sleeves rolled.

Every mango she clips hits the crate like a punch line with no laugh.

Burra cruises by on the quad, tyres kicking gravel. One flick of the clipboard - and two hours vanish from your payslip.

By 8 a.m., we're burning from the inside out. By 10, the air turns philosophical, testing whether sweat or shame evaporates faster.

———

Hamid, age eleven, has filled six crates already.

He nods at my bag: "Clip higher, Mister. Less ladder."

I thank him with what's left of my pride.

Shade break arrives.

But so does Dada, grinning like he invented unpaid overtime.

"Double quota tomorrow," he announces.

"Broome consignment stalled. Sleep fast."

. . .

Then he's gone. Just tyre tracks and that sticky, late-morning silence.

Back in the rows.

Gloves wet. Fingers numb. Latex dries into scales.

My crate count crawls. Burra rounds 20.8 kilos to nineteen without blinking.

By sundown, the orchard smells like cut fruit, sap, and resignation.

Rekha limps toward the weigh station. I follow, both of us part fruit, part ghost.

Dada's stopwatch is back in its pouch. But it hasn't stopped ticking.

———

Tomorrow: double quota.

Tonight: sleep on a rusted bunk.

Rest: accrues slowly. Paid in pain.

Out here, even recovery comes with conditions.

34 BLISTER PARADE

5:46 p.m.

The Kimberley doesn't do sunsets; it flambés them. One blink the sky's a blowtorch, next blink we're the marshmallows, blistered and collapsing on our own sticks. Row by row, we hobble toward the camp, mango latex drying into armour that doesn't protect a thing. Crates clunk down like overdue invoices. Every step costs a layer of skin, every breath tastes of sap and the kind of dust accountants can't write off.

Relief is exactly one bloodwood tree-shade shaped like a postage stamp, but to us it's world heritage. Joseph's already there, apron traded for a Broncos T-shirt faded to philosophical brown, dangling his latest invention: milk-carton bladders half-filled with ice. Kimberley cryotherapy.

. . .

"Ord Valley Spa, madam–sir," he croons, Tagalog vowels dipped in mischief. "Two-star hygiene, no waiting list."

He slaps the first bag onto Rekha's ankle. Steam ghosts up; her glasses fog, dignity doesn't. She grits out a laugh. "Mangosutra, deluxe package."

My turn: ice against palm blisters that look like I tried high-fiving the sun. Cold bites, nerves yelp, gratitude sulks. Behind us crates hiss as latex meets heat- orchard applause for human foolishness.

Noah and Jade- Miriwoong cousins with red dirt in their blood- drop beside us. Noah empties a bottle of warm water over his head, baptises himself in sweat run-off. "Sun's on penalty rates," he mutters. Jade rubs eucalyptus leaves to pulp, hands them over: "Smells like koala armpit, works like chemist." I smear the paste; it burns just enough to prove I'm alive.

Rahim shepherds Hamid and Noor into the shade. The boy's palms are raw, still clutching his fourth crate tag like a merit badge. Maryam follows, biro tucked behind ear-today she numbered every mango they picked so Burra can't magic them into thin air. Bureaucracy, meet maternal vengeance.

. . .

Joseph circulates: ice bag, joke, quick scribble in his black notebook **SINS & RECIPES**-today's entry reads *"22 crates docked 4 kg for sunshine tax."* Evidence marinating.

Burra's quad coughs smoke at the field edge. Clipboard flash. He counts heads, not souls. Revs once- dust settles on our hair, on our morale, on Joseph's improvised freezer section. Identity, now served with a crust.

Rekha flexes her ankle: swollen to cricket-ball size, throbbing like an unpaid bill. "Twenty-two crates tomorrow?" she asks nobody.

"Thirty," I answer. Dada back-dated a storm in Broome, upgraded our suffering.

Hamid pipes up, voice small but defiant. "We beat thirty," he says. Pride wrapped in gauze.

I swallow a laugh - the kid still believes math will rescue us. "We'll try," I say, and that lie is the softest thing my mouth can manage.

The sun finally slips below the irrigation pumps. Heat lingers- a memo, unpaid. Joseph collects the spent ice bags, a little ceremony for killed pain. "Dinner's yellow mystery," he announces. "Curry so bland it'll apologise for itself."

. . .

We push up, joints snapping like cheap pens. Latex cracks, fresh dust fills the seams: new résumé inked in blisters, signed in sweat. Ahead, the canteen glows fluorescent, promising carbs and more sarcasm. Behind, the bloodwood returns to silhouette duty, sap dripping slow-counting seconds until dawn whistles us back to row one.

Somewhere in that drip I hear the orchard laughing: soft hands, hard debt, repeat. I adjust the mesh bag strap across raw shoulder, offer Rekha an elbow. She takes it, stumbles once, keeps moving. No certificates here, just proof of endurance-pain stamped, ice-bag certified, ready for tomorrow's hiring committee: sun, quota board, and a stopwatch that never sleeps.

35 PLASTIC-FORK PHILOSOPHY

Ord Valley Orchard, Sunday, 11 March 2018

The orchard canteen isn't a room; it's a tin echo box.

Fluorescent jaundice overhead, detergent fumes thick enough to butter.

Dinner sweats in steel bain-maries.

Yellow Mystery on the left, Red Mystery on the right—Joseph's nightly choose-your-own surrender.

I grab a tray still glistening from its last regret.

Flies argue ownership of my shirt while I slide along the queue.

. . .

Janice stands guard, rice scoop flawless like airline service she'll never do again.

She taps a plastic fork on the bain-marie rim-tiny maestro cueing despair.

"Single-use cutlery, single-use people," she murmurs.

Snap-fork neck gone. "See? Bend once, bin forever. That's us, lah."

We migrate to a wobbling table.

Fluoro tubes click like arthritic knees; each buzz reminds the wiring it's on casual rates too.

Rekha parks opposite, ankle puffed beneath eucalyptus gauze.

She sizes up her fork as if it were a doomed bridge truss.

Noah arrives shining in sweat-salt jewellery, dumps two warm Cool Drinks.

"Hydrate or hallucinate." Jade follows, opens a bottle with her teeth- glamour clocked off.

Janice brandishes another fork.

"Know why management loves these?"

Snap- two halves. "Sterile, cheap, break before seconds."

The shards clink; the table hushes. Rahim's kids stare as if the plastic prophesies.

Burra barges in-quad helmet, clipboard, storm front.

Big man scans trays like inventory, a fly lands on his cheek and lives.

"Tomorrow: forty-crate average or find a bus ticket."

He smirks at a broken fork. "Quality gear-problem must be the operators."

Manila envelope-ABN carbon copies-thump. "Sign, don't whine."

Silence puddles. A zap-light claims a fly; spark sounds like applause.

Janice stacks fork fragments. "Disposable labour, lesson two."

She presses jagged ends; plastic bows, remembers the bend.

Pieces drop into Yellow Mystery, sink like rotten equity.

Rekha lifts a mango-shaped lump of Red Mystery.

"So what's the metal cutlery?" she asks.

.   .   .

"Citizenship," Janice fires back. "You still scratch pans, but at least they wash you."

Noah laughs into Cool Drink. "Metal's heavy- bosses hate postage."

Mariam rips flatbread, feeds Noor and Hamid.

"Metal holds heat," she murmurs. "Too dangerous to hold."

Joseph emerges, curry death-spatter on apron.

"Five-minute warning- kitchen closes faster than visa processing."

He pockets Janice's snapped fork. "Evidence bag."

Phone vibrates-Roy.

I kill the screen without glancing; Yellow Mystery reflects dust-ringed eyes back at me.

Hamid tries bending his fork; plastic snaps, half lands in rice.

He shrugs, keeps eating with the stump. Adaptation learned before algebra.

I raise my tray- silent toast. Kid grins orange.

Our generators outside grumble low-budget thunder.

Stars spark above rows of unseen mangoes, slicing distance-
Thomastown, Pampady, nowhere.

Predators recycle; plastic forks recycle.

Dinner off. Trays clatter, plates sluice.

Rekha pockets her slightly bent fork. "Souvenir. Proof we
were almost metal."

We limp into the hot dark, plastic prongs rattling like
counterfeit coins.

Lights snap off- single-use photons, tossed after shining once.

36 TIN-BOX CLINIC

Our cabin is a repurposed sardine tin, baking its way toward midnight.

Corrugated walls sweat rust. The swamp cooler wheezes sand.

Rekha's ankle has ballooned into a colour Dulux doesn't sell.

She tugs at her boot; the laces laugh and tighten.

Enter Mariam-Afghan, a matriarch in charity-shop hijab, carrying an enamel bowl, a scorched kettle, a strip of cotton hacked from yesterday's laundry.

She doesn't ask permission. She folds cross-legged. Metal clangs. Steam ghosts up like incense for lost causes.

. . .

"Salt first." Kabul dust in her voice, Javanese mildew in the edges.

Crystals sprinkle. Boiling water hisses. She stirs with a borrowed screwdriver.

The air shifts: half sea-breeze, half wound-care.

Rekha jokes about halal foot soup. Mariam snorts, dips the rag, wraps the ankle with nurse-school precision, the UN never funded.

Steam fogs Rekha's glasses; she blinks like someone reading bad news already suspected.

Hamid and Noor hover in the doorway, sticky palms, wide-angle eyes.

Mariam works, words soft so tin walls won't tattletale:

"Java crossing took two nights, six engines-four worked, two pretended."

Karachi brokers charged extra for cloudy weather.

Mid-channel the motor died; a man named Farid prayed louder than waves until the ocean prayed back with silence.

"Water everywhere," she knots the cloth, "but thirst the size of Australia."

. . .

Rekha's breath finds neutral.

I pass Joseph's milk-bag ice.

Mariam slides it under the wrap-salt, cold, eucalyptus locked in one desperate poultice.

Hamid steps forward, solemn as a customs beagle, hands over a half-melted barley sugar. "Painkiller."

Rekha salutes, peels plastic, lets grief and glucose dissolve together.

Mariam checks the arch-one beat, two. Satisfied the foot won't mutiny tonight.

"Tomorrow, elevate. And tell the quota man your ankle is Hazaragi. He'll underestimate it."

Flash of teeth-humour, or a border crossing in disguise.

I grope for payment-gratitude, money, illusion of safety, manage only a question: "Why trust us?"

She shrugs; the gesture costs nothing.

"Sea teaches: only strangers pull you onto the deck; family still screams on shore."

. . .

Kettle, screwdriver, dignity gathered, she shepherds the kids out.

Hamid presses a battered tube of antibiotic into my palm—boat-day pharmacy. "For blisters."

Generator hum swallows him.

Rekha flexes. Bandage holds; pain downgrades to weather report.

Tin roof pings. Geckos click Morse code no one will decode.

Top bunk: German backpacker snores through sunburn.

Outside: Burra's quad coughs once, territory marked.

Swamp cooler spits a final lukewarm sigh and dies.

Rekha finishes the barley sugar.

"National Health Service of Nowhere just saved my foot?"

"Better bedside manner than my Melbourne GP."

We laugh-quiet, careful-because tin remembers everything.

Her hand finds mine: sticky with sap, sweet with sugar, wrapped in someone else's courage.

Trust swapped, receipt waived.

37 ROSTER ROULETTE

Ord Valley Orchard, Tuesday, 13 March 2018

ABN, n. /ˌeɪ.biːˈɛn/ - *Australian Business Number*.

1. An eleven-digit identifier issued by the Commonwealth so a real or imagined enterprise can invoice, be taxed, or be fined.

2. Colloq.: a sheet of paper that turns a human into a line item nobody has to roster or remember.

———

Bulletin board used to list quotas.

Today it lists roulette.

Overnight edits

• Germans shunted to Block 8 - more shade, fewer witnesses.

• Indonesians scattered so Bahasa can't unionise.

• Rahim's family sliced three ways for "productivity diversity."

• Rekha and I upgraded to **Row Zero**, where the sun clocks in first and the water truck files for leave.

Burra prowls with a sheaf of **neon-green ABN forms**.

Hands them out like border cops handing please-explain slips.

"Congrats, you're a business now." Clipboard thumps ribcages.

Form perfume: cheap toner & expensive consequences.

Clause 3 - *I am an independent contractor, therefore allergic to overtime, sick leave, empathy.*

Signature box roomy enough to bury a payslip.

Dada lounges on the HiLux bonnet, stopwatch ticking like a Geiger counter.

"Paperwork makes equals of us all," he crows.

Orchard dialect: some of you starve at different tax rates.

Burra translates into two verbs: **Sign. Move.**

Hesitate? Pen jab to sternum.

Can't read English? Copy the swirl he traces in the dust, identity reduced to decorative loop.

Hamid, eleven, tries giving the form back.

Burra shrugs: "Kid runs his own start-up now."

Rahim signs for him; the biro groans.

Mariam pockets her carbon copy the way you pocket live ammo.

My turn. Sheet weighs more than the snips.

Fine print: *The Principal bears no responsibility for visa compliance.*

Translation: When Immigration shows, Dada points at this paper and shrugs in gravity.

I sign. Orchard physics: Don't sign, you drop off tomorrow's roster, terminal velocity unrecorded.

Rekha signs the next three letters only, ink rationed like dignity.

Stack complete.

Burra fans the forms like a royal flush.

"Paperwork done. Rotations- effective now. Sun's wasting invoices."

Quad revs. Dust baptises our newborn enterprises.

Dada salutes with a stubby: "Soft hands, hard tax brackets!"

We scatter to alien rows, each a one-person company licensed to bleed.

Inside my skull a ledger updates:

income tax I'll never see back, super I'll never collect, skin I'll shed to keep pace with a law that reclassifies sweat as entrepreneurship.

Paper hasn't freed us; it's just moved the chains to a new column- capital expenditure, depreciating daily.

Mesh bag over shoulder.

Ink of my autograph dries- title deed to my own exploitation.

Row Zero waits, sun ready to audit the first drip of collateral.

38 BREAK IN ECHO

Ord Valley Orchard, Monday, 14 March 2018

10:38 p.m.

Generator lullaby just slipped into second gear, swamp-cooler spit tickling the tin roof, when my phone vibrates hard enough to rattle the bunk.

One blurry bar.

Caller ID: **KARTIK, MELB**.

Thomastown is three time zones east, but the panic in that ringtone crosses deserts faster than Optus.

"Karti-"

"They came, bro."

His voice is shredded balloon rubber.

"Some hoodlums - Vietnamese, Arabs, I don't know. Three of them. Front door kicked in at 3 a.m. Your old room first. Then Zainab's."

The cabin temperature drops ten degrees.

Rekha, half-asleep on the top bunk, props up on one elbow.

Her shadow hangs like a question mark in sweat-stained pyjamas.

It has to be Trang.

That guy doesn't know how to let go.

I once heard he kept a GPS tag in a girlfriend's bike seat - *"for her safety."*

When she ghosted him, he tracked her halfway to Canberra, then deleted her contact and added her brother to the payroll.

Trang wasn't a gangster - he was worse: a businessman with abandonment issues.

Loyalty, to him, was a contract carved into your thighs.

You didn't exit his orbit; you got spun into a darker one.

The padded envelope to Detective Price must've reached its consequences.

No return address. No fingerprints. Just a thumb drive and a note: *Loose end, not confession.*

Looks like Trang took it personally.

Took it as the ultimate betrayal.

Trang has people - even if they don't know they're his yet.

And someone always needs A$ 200 more than they need peace.

"Zainab okay?"

"Hysterical but breathing. They rough-handled, called her curry-something, demanded your new address. Found the Kununurra flyer you stuck on the fridge."

Post-it breadcrumbs, meet wolves.

"They steal anything?"

"My laptop, her phone, probably Gaurav's dignity. Smashed the router, too - message sent. Zainab's filing police tomorrow. They carved a mango into your pillow, dude - knife art. 'PAY WHAT YOU OWE.' Spelt 'owe' with a zero."

· · ·

A laugh sidles up my throat. Dies.

Out here I dodge quota knives; in Thomastown my absence is a burglary accessory.

"Police will ask why international students keep attracting machete karaoke," I mutter.

Kartik wheezes.

"Funny thing - cops already suspect a 'bike-theft syndicate link.' I think your name's still on their sticky note."

Of course it is.

Identity is Velcro for accusations that fit the skin.

Generator hiccups; swamp-cooler coughs one last breath.

Dies.

Tin roof sighs like a closing coffin.

"Kart - keep receipts, screenshot everything, get Zainab a hotel on my card."

(My card balances on mango crates and borrowed breath, but guilt underwrites credit.)

He exhale-laughs.

"Bro, you're picking fruit in Mordor. How's your card still alive?"

"Don't ask; don't decline."

I promise call-backs. Hang up.

Screen reads **Battery: 9%**.

Signal dissolves to zero - Melbourne, Thomastown, Trang.

All ghosted by geography.

Rekha's voice drops from the bunk:

"Bad news?"

"Melbourne growing new teeth," I say.

"Sharp ones."

She pauses, then:

"Every place rots, given the right humidity."

We lie there, listening to the generator's distant snore, the orchard leaves hissing gossip outside the mesh.

Thomastown was meant to be the safe chapter - the beige suburb that held our original selves in bubble wrap.

Tonight bubble wrap popped.

Identity, it turns out, has a melting point lower than mango sap.

But here's what Trang forgot:

People who send anonymous files know how to keep backups.

And people who owe Roy know how to survive storms.

I've been watching this orchard.

Not for hours - for days.

I've seen rosters rewritten in pencil.

Bins sealed before inspections.

Boys from Darwin paid in vouchers.

Rekha's shift doubled and still docked.

Bruce vomiting after mystery spray.

Marisol walking funny, saying nothing.

Dada thinks fear is fertilizer.

But fear, long enough, grows a spine.

.   .   .

Tomorrow I'll fake a bathroom break and photograph the pay sheets.

The next day I'll map the supply shed's late-night loading.

By Friday, I'll have enough to be dangerous-or valuable.

New folder: **Sunripe_Archive.**

I won't call it revenge.

Just... preservation.

Inside, I update my private ledger:

Flight risk: +1

Retaliation buffer: +50

Witness value: under construction.

39 EVIDENCE COLLECTED

Ord Valley Orchard, Thursday, 15 March 2018

2:57 p.m.

Burra calls the shipping container **"the office."**

It's really a mausoleum for payroll sins- stale Skoal, capitalism left to rot in 42-degree shade.

I arrive with a requisition chit for toilet paper-two-roll ration per entrepreneur.

Tucked under my shirt: one wheezy Android, cracked lens, just enough battery to commit treason.

Fluoro tubes buzz like guilty teeth.

Folding table sags beneath cash tin and carbon-copy towers.

Burra hunches, pen scalping numbers:

• Rahim's **24** crates → **21**.

• Mariam's signature scraped off, stapled to phantom "R. Fernandez."

• Every kilo over minimum fed to ghosts who never sweat.

I drift left, study an OSHA poster older than Google.

Click-monitor: spreadsheet tab *ADJUSTED YIELDS*.

Click-clipboard: columns *Actual* vs *Invoiceable*.

Click-drawer of passports: Indonesian, Hazara, one Nepali sharing Rekha's surname.

Tiny mosquito flashes. Guilt hums louder than the ballast.

Burra slurps iced coffee, oblivious.

Two-way radio sputters static country in the corner.

I collect my toilet rolls, camouflage loot, and back-pedal into glare.

Behind the water tank: one bar of signal, drunk on its own altitude.

Telegram pops; Joseph's burner @Sins&Recipes waits.

Photos launch skyward- ghost workers, stolen kilos, passport vault.

Green ticks bloom; evidence now parked on an AWS server that charges less interest than Roy.

Signal dies. Mission filed.

Cabin 7 reeks of eucalyptus and yesterday's panic.

Rekha rereads a pathology textbook she no longer believes.

She eyes the toilet paper. "Stockpiling for siege?"

"Evidence collection."

She doesn't probe; trust is our last untaxed commodity.

Outside, Dada guns the HiLux; stopwatch ticks like a fraud metronome.

Sap drips, crates fill, but tonight a packet of pixels rides visa-free toward someone who still remembers what a whole wage looks like.

40 WRONG PICKUP

Ord Valley Orchard, Friday, 16 March 2018

11:08 a.m.

Block 6 was all oven-heat and latex sting until a HiLux clattered in with a stranger riding shotgun - thin frame, city fade tucked beneath a borrowed Akubra.

Trang.

Burra only saw free muscle.

"New Indo lot?" he barked, stabbing the clipboard toward the dust.

Trang blinked, halfway to correcting him - **"Vietnam-"**

. . .

Burra didn't listen.

Mesh bag to the ribs.

"Row Eight. Twenty crates before lunch, Curry-bro."

Trang flicked the clipboard back reflexively - wrong dialect for this postcode.

Burra's grin stopped moving.

Crack. Forearm like a fence post.

Thud. Steel-toe to thigh.

Trang swung the mesh bag. Unripe mangoes smacked meat.

Burra's radio squawked - ignored.

He fisted Trang's collar, heaved him into the ute tray - classed as produce now - then gunned it behind the rumbling gut of the farm's thirstiest engine.

Where complaints go to compost.

I followed at coward's distance.

Sap seared my arms.

My phone jittered in my pocket.

Soundtrack: boots. Mango thumps. One wet snap.

. . .

Trang fought to the last - thumb in Burra's eye, spit in his beard - until a final knee made silence leak out of him.

Burra emerged, wiping red knuckles on a payroll docket.

"Soft hands," he muttered.

Clipboard update:

Inbound 'Trang-something' - quit without notice.

No passport recorded. No exit interview.

The quad roared off in search of new bodies.

I crouched.

Pulse? One flutter - tax file: zero.

Latex sap dripped onto his cheek.

The orchard signing its own death certificate.

Phone flash:

Face. Blood. Abandonment.

Pixel proof.

Enough to outlive deniability.

Then back to Row 6.

Snips shaking.

Crates still gaping.

But that's the thing about enemies of enemies.

They don't come bearing knives or apologies - they come wearing borrowed hats and bad timing.

Trang didn't come to pick fruit.

He came to find me.

To deliver a warning. Maybe a threat.

Instead, he got upgraded to casualty.

He survived a syndicate.

An arrest sweep.

Even me - mailing his empire to a detective with a note that said: *"Loose end, not confession."*

But he didn't survive Burra's quota rage.

One of us was supposed to die.

The orchard just flipped a coin.

I should feel relieved.
Instead, I feel late -
like I showed up to my own reckoning with the wrong script.

I didn't kill Trang.
But I put him in the line of sight.
I didn't hold the mattock. But I let the dirt cover him.

Enemies don't cancel each other out.
They just become proof that survival is about **timing**, not **virtue**.

And right now, **timing** is the only thing still on my side.
For now.

41 MANGO BLOOD

Ord Valley Orchard, Wednesday, 21 March 2018

11:46 a.m.

Behind Shed Three, the world shrinks to corrugate, generator hum, and a rectangle of dirt that never applied for grave duty.

Burra swings the mattock like he's cracking open a stubborn paycheck -

each thump spitting sap into the air, flicking mango pulp off his boots.

Trang lies nearby -

face half-covered by the same mesh bag that failed promotion from produce to person.

Unripe fruit roll out, leaking latex and something darker.

Orchard juice meets artery juice -

same colour, once Kimberley dust salts it.

I stay in the weed fringe, spine pressed to a rain tank that reeks of rust and algae.

Snapshot's already in my phone's encrypted gut.

Now I log the after-shot:

hole depth, weapon of choice, Burra's kill posture - chin up, belly swinging like a grandfather clock of indifference.

Burra stops to spit.

Wipes his brow with Trang's shirt.

Rolls the body slow. Practised.

Bones clack.

The sound yanks me back to Thomastown:

blue tarp, cracked helmet, Karthik's whisper-

they want your address.

Geography pulls.

Survival grips.

Plastic sacks follow -

bad fruit, half-melted ice, a passport Trang never had time to open.

Evidence, composted.

Burra whistles a '90s country tune about dust and paradise.

The grave hits knee-depth.

Policy here prefers speed over symbolism.

He drops a rusted drum lid as a headstone.

Shovels erase shoes, then face, then the blinking earpiece still muttering SOS.

I breathe through my shirt.

Silence tastes like mango vinegar.

Burra lights a Winfield, kicks the mound like it's late paperwork.

No prayer.

No clock-out beep.

Just exhaust syntax and a clipboard waiting for its next correction.

Count to ten.

Nothing moves but a crow.

It lands. Looks. Leaves.

I step forward.

Boot tip presses the mound.

Soil's still warm - illusion of life.

One more photo:

Grave. Crow. Partial bloody footprint.

Burra's size-eleven call-signature.

I don't rebury the evidence.

I rebury the urge to speak.

Orchard code is clear:

The mouth that opens gets reassigned to a hole of its own.

Pixels travel faster than testimony.

Bruise slower. Burn deeper.

I dust bootprints with a branch -

old cricket reflex, hiding ball marks so the game could stretch
past curfew.

By the time I reach Row Zero, the sun's reheated morality to
pliable.

Rekha sees my face, starts to ask -

I answer with crates:

Lift. Drop. Tag. Repeat.

Words can wait for signal bars.

Right now, survival is an action verb.

Silence, its grammatical tense.

Shed Three recedes behind foliage -

just another secret planted in Kimberley soil.

Latex drips down my wrists.

Mango blood. Human blood.

Still sweet to the flies.

Still invisible to quotas.

42 DIESEL CONFESSION

Ord Valley Orchard, Thursday, 22 March 2018

Night welds the cabin shut. Fumes hum lullabies in the yard when Rekha drops her question like a bolt cutter.

"How deep did they bury him?"

No preamble- she's already read the truth on my skin the way mango sap brands latex.

I wait for the swamp cooler to drown in its phlegm.

"Shallow enough," I say. "A good rain'll vote him back up."

. . .

She sits on the lower bunk, ankle bandage glowing sulphur under the safety light.

"And you?" she asks. Voice flat as a field report. "You just watched?"

I think about spinning silence into nobility- pixels, proof, survival math. But the orchard's sandblasted that out of me.

"I watched," I say. "Photographed. Then shut up. Burra's mattock doesn't do feedback."

She opens Joseph's ice chest, scoops melting cubes into a cup, presses them to her ankle.

"Cowardice in HD," she mutters. "You documented a murder so the cloud could feel informed."

I flare. "One upload means Burra can't rewrite the ledger-"

"Upload?"

She slaps the cup down. Ice clatters like a busted jaw.

·   ·   ·

"Trang's ledger ended in exhaust and topsoil. Yours is still a draft folder."

It stings. Because it's true. Because it's her.

Outside: Dada's HiLux idles near the shed. Blue headlights slice the dust. We hear the clink of his stubby, clipboard latch creaking.

Rekha tilts her head, counting seconds like a bomb tech.

"He's moving bodies," she whispers. Crates. Quotas. Ghosts.

Then she stands. Favours her ankle. Pulls a biro from her ponytail.

On the back of a freight docket she sketches: sheds, fuel drums, water tanks.

"Tomorrow you pick. I wander. We build a map. Every stash, every whisper Joseph gives us."

She circles Shed Three. A noose in blue ink.

. . .

"Evidence that breathes," she says. "Not the kind waiting in Dropbox for someone's courage subscription to renew."

I stare at her. Half-ashamed. Half relieved, someone still believes planning beats panic.

She hands me the pen.

"Your turn," she says. "Plot tonight's grave. Depth, distance, tree marker. If the rain unearths him, we hand coordinates to the cops."

I mark an X. The biro judders over plywood. My pulse slows for the first time since the burying.

She caps the pen. "We out-think Dada or we fertilise the mangoes. Choose."

Generator coughs back to life. Floodlights ignite. Orchard rows glow military neat, crimes hidden under chlorophyll.

I fold the map. Slide it into the busted mattress spring.

She nods. Pact sealed in mildew.

•   •   •

I reach for her hand. Sap crust still lines my knuckles. She takes it anyway. Palm warm. Wrist thrumming.

"Courage," she says, "is just fear that remembers the exit code."

Engine breath leaks under the door, mixing with eucalyptus and the metal tang of vows struck on the cheap.

We sit on the bunk, listening to the ute idle. Somewhere out there, under mango branches, a shallow grave waits for rain.

Above it, two stubborn hearts redraw the orchard, line by lethal line.

43 DOUBLE-QUOTA DAY

Sun clocks in early, brandishing a blowtorch.

Dada meets it halfway: **"Forty crates each or discover your inner hunger artist."**

He reads the laminate like gospel; we're apostates on parole.

Burra backs him with a pallet of mesh bags, extra-wide straps, and deeper shoulder trenches.

Shed-Two thermometer fakes 39 °C; plastic only warps past forty.

Sap turns leaves to chlorophyll glue.

Clip, spray, instant scabs.

Gloves become boiled prawns.

Rekha's taped ankle throbs Morse code: *unpaid-leave*.

———

Row 15, crate 7

Hamid-eleven-ghosts by.

"Up high, Mister-bigger fruit."

Bag half his body, grin half his religion.

Tree bleeds me instead.

Row 23, crate 14

Noah's rash draws maps- red continents across skin.

Footy chant whistles, dies mid-lyric.

Jade hands rusted bottle; half evaporates on exit.

Row 30, crate 22

Sky tilts, film splice broken.

Burra drifts on quad, clipboard docking kilos.

Mariam's count rounded down; carbon-copy mafia rolls on.

Shade break? Six minutes.

"Productivity protocol," Dada says, chugging electrolytes we'll never taste.

Joseph's milk-bag ice liquefies faster than apologies.

Rekha lifts ankle; bandage amber with sap and stubborn blood.

Numbers answer her: 42 °C, 18 crates, zero sympathy.

———

Back out. Mangoes glow radioactive.

Latex spits halos; we clip by Braille.

Burra hollers, "Hydrate, idiots," docks Rahim another kilo for sweaty handwriting.

Row 42, crate 36

Jade folds- knees like budget tents.

Face meets dust. Breath exits.

Silence louder than the quad.

Dada rolls up, stopwatch ticking empathy debt.

Joseph slides ice under her neck; docket reads: **CRATE TOTAL 23 - LEFT FIELD.**

Optional lunch break, apparently.

We stand- malfunctioning scarecrows awaiting permission to fall.

The sun audits us harder than payroll ever will.

None issued.

·   ·   ·

Row 47, crate 39

Rekha's ankle yelps; strap knots tighter.

Mariam hums boat- lullaby pace; Hamid drums fruit into crates.

Row 50, crate 40

I tag the last box, wrists seizing, shaking.

Burra weighs: **20.2 kg → 19**.

"Quality shrinkage," he grins.

Forty becomes thirty-nine. Ledger bleeds another kilo of unpaid sweat.

———

Evening limps in; thermometer insists 41.

Crates drag to weigh-station-war trophies, no one asked for.

Jade cooling in the canteen fridge; survival accepts PayPal.

Her debt is reassigned to us tomorrow, interest compounds.

Dinner = Red Mystery in futility marinade.

One fork per two souls. Single-use, double solidarity.

Rekha stirs without appetite: **"Body as wallet-spent before lunch."**

· · ·

Phone vibrates-Roy: **EXIT FEE ages like cheese, da.**

Sweat interest meets rupee interest; both compound despair.

Burra's shadow tallies bodies against tomorrow's math.

Stars unseen, latex ghosts sigh.

I file new deficits to photo cache: kilos docked, bodies collapsed, climate charging late fees.

Sleep will loan itself in instalments- repayable at dawn, compounding by sunrise.

Contract signed in sap: forty crates, 42 °C, one body on the dirt, ledger still hungry.

44 SIGNAL HILL

The orchard sleeps like a crime scene - quiet, but you can smell what happened.

We move between mango rows, headlamps off, moon bleaching everything hospital white.

Destination: Signal Hill. The only place in fifty kilometres where your phone gets more than a shrug.

Rekha limps beside me, ankle taped tight, jaw tighter.

The mesh bag she carries isn't full of mangoes - just a phone, a USB drive, and one melted Snickers.

The air's thick enough to chew. Every step peels sweat and pesticide off our backs.

. . .

Halfway up she mutters, "Hill's taller when your foot hates you."

I offer a piggyback.

She gives me a glare sharp enough to sterilise the dirt.

We reach the top. Ten metres of altitude, half a kilometre of distance.

Two bars appear on my screen. That's all we need.

I open the encrypted folder:

• Photos of docked kilo sheets

• Jade's collapse record

• Trang's murder: blood pooled near Shed Three, timestamped

• The bootprint I traced in the red dirt after

Rekha holds the phone steady. I hit upload.

All of it goes to @Sins&Recipes - the shared cloud folder Joseph set up.

Green ticks fire off like tiny verdicts.

Once we're sure everything's sent, I type the message that matters most:

"Photos of Trang. Heat casualty log. New file dump complete."

Then I forward it directly to Joseph's backup number - the one he gave me the night Burra's math didn't add up.

Five seconds later: **Delivered.**

Ten more: **Read.**

That's our signal. Not knocks on a wall. Not metaphor.

Upload = contact. Read = confirmation.

We sit on a granite slab. Below us, the orchard glows faint - generators humming, Dada's ute parked near the crates.

The place looks calm. It isn't.

Rekha unwraps her bandage slowly, breath steady.

She doesn't speak for a while. Then:

We sit on a slab of granite.

Below us, the orchard glows faint fumes buzzing, Dada's ute, a grid of wage theft wrapped in fairy lights.

Rekha unwraps her bandage slowly, breath steady.

She doesn't speak for a while. Then:

"I told my aunt once."

I wait.

"About Dev. About what happened in Pokhara. Not everything - just enough to need help."

She pulls a loose thread from the edge of the bandage. Doesn't look at me.

"She put her hand on my head like I was sick. Said maybe it was a bad dream. Said not to tell anyone else - not friends, not teachers, not even cousins."

She flicks the thread into the dust.

"Then she made me promise not to talk about it again. Not even to her."

Silence stretches out. I don't try to fill it.

· · ·

"After that, I stopped explaining. Even now, if Dev walks near me in Melbourne, I just... disappear."

Her voice tightens.

"Because what do you do with something everyone tells you didn't happen?"

The wind lifts a corner of the foil wrapper from the Snickers bar.

She presses it down with one finger.

Then, looking out at the grid below:

"That's why this stuff?" She taps the phone. "The photos, the logs, the blood... We can't let it vanish. Not this time. Not into some aunt's drawer or Burra's bin."

I nod.

"Evidence shouldn't disappear into corners."

"Exactly," she says.

"Because silence doesn't protect you. It just stores you. For later."

We check the phone one more time.

Files sent. Backup secured.

Joseph knows.

Let the record show: we said something.

———

Friday, 30 March · 6:37 p.m.

Canteen after shift is a bad dream reheated:

Rice glue, generator hum, and one fly arguing with the light.

Joseph hands me a tray of curry, then slides something else across:

A black pocket notebook, cover torn, grease-stained, held together by sheer will.

Gold marker reads:

SINS & RECIPES

.   .   .

"Kitchen closes in five," he says, voice flat.

"Read quick."

I duck into the pantry and flip through:

1 FEB – Jade: 17 crates, docket says 15

3 FEB – Rahim: 24 reported, 21 paid. "Evaporation" excuse.

5 FEB – Fake ID 'R. Fernandez' paid A$ 420

Every page screams: stolen wages, ghost workers, falsified dockets.

Margin notes include dinner prep like side-dish instructions:

Diesel gravy / 50:1 rice ratio / Serve with lie

Joseph appears behind the door.

"Cop's cousin loves my adobo," he says.

"Hates Burra's numbers. These hit his inbox tonight."

"Why give this to me?"

He shrugs.

"Every crusade needs a backup martyr. You're already bleeding - might as well bleed loud."

I flip to today's entry:

• Jade: Heat Casualty #2

• Trang: **Name logged. Circled.**

• Status: **Body?**

I pick up the pen.

"15 MAR – Trang. Buried Shed 3. Witness: A.N."

Joseph takes the notebook back like it's radioactive.

"Two more file dumps," he says.

"Then this place burns."

He's gone before I reply.

Outside, Burra's laughing at something no one remembers.

Dada's counting crates like they're rosary beads.

Neither of them sees the pantry door swinging closed.

· · ·

I finish my tray in three bites.

It tastes like cumin and subpoenas.

The notebook image stays with me.

So does the hill.

So does her voice.

This time, the evidence arrived.

This time, we didn't stay quiet.

45 BLUE LIGHTS IN THE MANGOES

Ord Valley Orchard, Tuesday, 3 April 2018

5:18 a.m.

Sirens, not engines, pull the orchard awake.

Blue strobes carve mango rows into police-line geometry.

First vehicle: **Australian Border Force chevrons.**

Second: **Fair Work crests.**

Third: **NT Police,** looking sorry for being punctual.

A drone hums overhead - bureaucracy's halo on lithium batteries.

Burra staggers out of the shipping-container "office," steel-capped half-laced.

A midnight-blue officer raises the politest assault rifle in WA.

"ID?"

Driver's licence handed over.

Clipboard man mispronounces twice, scrawls **BURROW** on the seizure sheet.

Cabin doors eject half-dressed pickers, dreams still evacuating.

Fair Work officers herd us by language clusters:

• "Indo" → left,

• "Viet" → right,

• "Subcontinent" → under the jacaranda that hasn't bloomed since Howard.

Rahim yells, **"Minors!"**

Hamid becomes **HAMLET.**

Noor: **NOR.**

Mercy: not on the form.

Dada strides up, stopwatch swinging - costume change late.

NT sergeant hands him a warrant thick as a mango crate.

His eyebrows attempt escape. Fail.

. . .

Padlock snapped.

Passport shoebox vomits its contents - counterfeit rainbow.

Rekha stands beside me, counting cruisers: two ABF, one Fair Work, four NT.

An agent mangles her name into **"RAY-KAR."**

She corrects.

He writes **"RICA."**

Identity drops a vowel but keeps the bill.

Fingerprint parade begins.

Barcode wristbands issued.

Mine ends in **212-BROWN** - a paint swatch nobody ordered.

Portable floodlight ignites the weigh station.

Crates glow radioactive.

Officers snip latex-wet stems, bag evidence rich in vitamin C.

Joseph, hairnet halo, hands instant coffee to a cop.

Winks: **cloud dump confirmed.**

Janice films cops filming crates - meta-justice vi A$ 99 Android.

Noah asks if seized mangoes count toward quota.

The officer almost smiles. Almost.

Humour not box-ticked.

7:03 a.m. - first arrest.

Not Dada.

Yet.

Recruiter **Gus**, charge: **unlicensed labour hire**.

The orchard fence suddenly looks shorter to its owner.

ABF bus loads half the workers for **"interview in town."**

Translation: **prove your latitude.**

Mariam boards with her kids, spine straight.

She taps three knocks on the window.

Our code - affidavit in Morse - ricochets off the tinted glass.

Paper cyclone begins:

Wrong names. Right fingerprints.

Heat takes over.

Blue lights dim.

Crates wait.

Sap drips.

No snips lifted.

Burra sits on an esky reading his misspelled charge sheet - learning gravity upside-down.

Dada clutches his stopwatch.

Seconds, suddenly, are heavy.

Somewhere under Shed Three, **Trang keeps silent**.

The ledger still lists him **"missing."**

But today, the **margins scream** loud enough for the law to hear.

8:44 a.m.

Scanner pings like a microwave.

"Nair, Arjun Ajith - Condition 8202 breach. Forty-seven days of non-attendance."

. . .

The officer doesn't even look up.

The printer curls out a notice - warm, yellow, already damning.

He staples it to a clipboard labelled **CLOCK 8022 -**

same code they slap on stray mango crates.

Outside, generators roar.

Handcuffs clink.

Dada's hierarchy collapses in stereo.

I pocket the crumpled carbon copy while his back is turned.

Ink still wet.

Destiny pre-stamped: **"Review: Deportation Possible."**

Forty-seven skipped lectures weigh less than one laminated mango -

but lighter things have broken spines.

46 VANISH POINT

Ord Valley Orchard, Thursday, 5 April 2018

9:06 p.m.

By dusk, the blue lights had packed up - Burra, Gus, and three ute-loads of evidence bound for Kununurra lock-up.

Dada, however, melted between clipboard flashes - one moment barking for a lawyer, the next, a HiLux tailgate creaked, and he was negative space in the floodlight. Rumour has him hiding in Wyndham, or halfway to Broome on the mango freight, or coiled in Shed Three's rafters like mouldy rope, waiting to be remembered. Silence signs every theory.

The orchard feels amputated. No stopwatch metronome. No sermons. Only sap dripping steady as a hospital IV. What's left of us gathers under the bloodwood - wages frozen, quotas cancelled, adrenaline on back-order. ABF has scheduled visa triage for dawn. Translation: prove a legal right to breathe or accept a complimentary ride to Perth detention.

Joseph paces with a wooden spoon, clutching it like a rosary of burnt hours.

"Boss ran, blame trickles downhill," he mutters, stirring imaginary curry.

Janice inventories options: "Protection visa, bridging visa, no-way-Jose visa."

Hamid tries the word bridging on his tongue; it sounds like brittle when a kid says it.

Rekha sits on an overturned crate, ankle still swollen, paperwork folder tighter than any tourniquet.

"Dada was our sponsor of record," she says. "No sponsor, no subclass 408, no nothing."

She laughs once - a cracked-dash sound.

"We're refugees from an MBA now."

Noah suggests phoning the union.

Jade reminds him that unions need membership fees, and we've been paid mostly in debt.

. . .

Mariam folds passport photocopies into the kids' socks - insurance against clipboard confiscation.

The generator coughs, dies.

Darkness inks the orchard. Every torch flickers on faces searching for the new org chart of survival.

Without Dada, who counts as the boss?

Without payslips, who qualifies as worker?

Identity here was always written in kilo ink.

Now the ledger has no author.

I hold the phone, battery at 12%.

Scroll the missed calls from Roy, the unread threats from "Unknown Private."

Predators go feral when prey changes postcodes.

I pocket the device.

If signals can vanish, so can I.

Joseph breaks the hush.

"Tomorrow ABF will ask: name, date of birth, employer."

He taps his spoon on his palm.

"We tell them employer evaporated - so did the employment."

He looks at me, then Rekha.

"Maybe we are customers now - consumers of mango injustice."

Rekha snorts.

"Can we return the product?"

Nobody laughs. The warranty expired with Dada's number plate.

We disperse to cabins that suddenly echo.

I lie on the bunk and watch geckos hunt moths with more certainty than any immigration officer will show us at sunrise.

Sleep edges in, carrying terms and conditions I don't bother to read.

Somewhere beyond Block 8, a HiLux engine turns over, growls once, then goes silent.

Could be Dada testing escape routes.

Could be orchard ghosts reheating menace.

· · ·

Either way, dawn will audit the living and the missing,
stamping **present** or **remove** on whatever bodies line up.

Tonight we're stuck in inventory limbo:

fruit without boxes, labour without labels, visas without
vowels.

No barcodes. No expiry dates.

Just people left over after the quota's been filled.

If Dada is the vanish point,

we are the smudged lines left behind -

waiting to see whether the law traces us back into shape or
erases us for good.

47 HARDWOOD BALANCE SHEET

Ord Valley Orchard, Thursday, 5 April 2018

5:20 a.m.

No ute.

No stopwatch glare.

No Dada.

Two dawns since the raid, and the orchard hangs in suspended sentence-

mangoes ripening, pickers moth-stunned, Burra telling investigators **dunno, mate**.

Word on the rows: police vans are still parked at the highway turn-off,

waiting for fugitives who can spell their own names.

And if they can't spell, the cuffs still fit.

Rule of flight:

When the boss disappears, your face climbs to the top of every clipboard.

We need passports.

We need wages.

We need out.

Fear's no longer panic - it's logistics now:

What to carry.

Who to trust.

How to vanish without echo.

Rekha doesn't speak, but her bag is packed.

Mine is half-zipped: USB backed up, burner charged, Trang's blood still cached in cloud memory.

The plan isn't dramatic.

It's surgical.

We're not stealing anything.

We're taking what they stole from us - wages withheld, names erased, silence taxed.

Then we walk.

Not for justice.

Just distance.

Rekha's ankle is mummified in eucalyptus tape; my fingers blister-wrapped.

We ghost past cabins where generators hiccup in their sleep.

Someone whispers, "They've got sniffer dogs" Someone else mutters ", Just cyclone rumours."

Either way, time's bleeding.

We know where to go.

Shed-Two is a plywood coffin – machinery, mildew, and overtime filed under silence.

The cash drawer exhales like last call at a dying pub.

Brick-wads wink in torchlight - mango-sticky, but crisp enough to ransom a postcode.

First bundle triggers a memory:

Week one. Dada flicking a rubber-band stack, docking two kilos, laughing:

"Advance, soft hands - real pay comes later."

Later never arrived.

Rekha plants herself in the doorway, torch between teeth, ankle twitching.

I shovel notes into a fertiliser sack until it weighs like betrayal.

Middle shelf coughs up ledgers: **PAY 17-18**, **ABN CONTRACTS**, **GHOSTS** - plus a USB marked **ATO BACKUP**.

Phone flash. Paper + polymer = severance package from hell.

Rough tally:

A$ 28,000. Two ledgers. One USB.

Shoebox of "spare" passports.

Owed wages, hazard pay, hush money.

Call it mango reparations.

Sack cinched. Door locked.

Mission half-done.

Then: headlights.

HiLux idling, engine breathing like a caged bull.

Dada slides out - no stubby, no stopwatch.

Boning knife: yes.

VB fumes ghost his breath.

"Funny thing about whistle-blowers," he rasps.

"They squeak."

He's stone-sober.

Which is the worst kind of drunk.

First lunge - blade skims ribs, shirt shreds, skin intact.

Second - knife punches plywood. Sticks.

Wood splinters like cheap promises.

I dive.

Grab a pallet plank - splinters baptise my palm.

Swing #1: knocks the blade wide.

His elbow clips my ear. Static detonates.

We circle-sap, grit, hard breathing.

I notice stupid details: split thumbnail.

Gold wedding band dented, caught on callus.

Human, once.

Clinch. Wrist-lock.

Knife clatters into the dark.

Shoulder drive - crates implode.

Latex splashes like bile.

Plank reclaimed.

Swing #2: edge across cheek. Blood, not surrender.

Tackle. Tumble.

Kidney kick. Rib bruise.

Parity of pain.

Up again under moonlight.

Swing #3: collarbone crack.

His fist lands. Stars bloom.

Swing #4: temple - ripe fruit pop.

He staggers but claws, muttering rent-collector curses.

Last swing - downstroke, full shoulder, centre skull.

Wet thunk no audit covers. Life invoices. Balance: zero.

Heartbeat hammer.

My fingers won't unclench the plank.

Ears ring like Myki alarms.

Pulse check: flutter... stall... silence.

Stopwatch in his pocket obeys gravity -

tick - tick - gone.

Rekha's torch slices panic into plans.

Cash. Ledgers. Five minutes.

Knife kicked under sacks.

Prints wiped with burlap.

Kimberley heat deputised for cleanup.

I catch myself shaking.

Adrenaline tastes metallic.

HiLux keys jingle like ransom.

Sack thuds into the tray.

.   .   .

Moon draws a shaky white line toward Highway 1.

Far off, heat lightning stitches the horizon - storm season sharpening its teeth.

Back in the cab, we drive with headlamps off.

Red dirt ghosts behind us, swallowed by night.

Behind us, Shed-Two seals its second secret in four days.

Crows will audit at dawn.

Ledger update, whispered between clenched teeth:

Debt to Roy - pending.

Police radius - closing.

Interest on fear - paid in hardwood.

Road ahead: Broome or bust.

Before the sun can sign its witness statement.

FILE FOUR
വഴിതാറ് · VAZHITHĀRU
HIGHWAY

Broome: red-rust roads, a motel floorboard safe, and the fork where Rekha and I fracture.

48 RED-DUST EXIT

Great-Northern Highway, Friday, 6 April 2018

4:20 a.m.

Ute guzzles its last mouthful of diesel, gauge blinking **COURTROOM RED** thirty k short of Halls Creek.

We nose it behind a termite mound, wipe prints, crack the number plates with a crowbar. Evidence now carrion for the heat.

Torch check: sack of orchard cash, ledgers, passport shoebox—all present, all sweating guilt.

Road unfurls black and empty, night insects auditioning for apocalypse.

· · ·

Rule of Thumb: Every fifth vehicle stops if you look broke but non-rabid.

Ride #1 – Sand-blasted **LandCruiser**, two dingoes in the tray, driver Tash, skin tanned to archival leather.

She accepts fuel money, rejects conversation, drops us at a roadhouse smelling of yesterday's chip fat and rationed freedom. Clock above the fryer: **7:03 a.m**.

Snack-bar Wi-Fi: one bar.

ABC headline loads slow, like shame buffering-**"Slave-Labour Orchard Probe Widens."**

Burra's mug shot pixelates into focus. I screenshot, file under *Karma - Processing*.

Corner store sells burner Nokias, no ID required.

$200 note, one already-alive SIM. I save a single contact: **Rekha.**

Ride #2 – Road-train cab, rubber mats & loneliness. Driver **Stewie** lectures tyre psi, gifts lukewarm Coke.

Two hours later he veers to a mine site. We unload at a sign that offers two futures:

.   .   .

↑ **DARWIN 936**   → **BROOME 525**

Sun strafes the letters; heat rises like second thoughts.

We choose Broome-boats, rumoured, questions optional.

Every kilometre west feels less like escape, more like betting your life on a rumour with no return policy.

Ride #3 – **VAN-GABOND**, duct-tape calligraphy, Dutch couple chasing sunsets, ukulele bleeding Bluetooth chords.

Mandarins for breakfast, zero questions asked.

At Roebuck Plains, they hug goodbye like we're an extended warranty on their adventure.

Broome – 7:10 p.m.

Town smells of seaweed and hour-rental dreams.

First purchase: campground locker-combo **3-9-1** (Rekha's birthday).

Sack of hush money + ledgers + passports go inside. Metal door shuts like a vault on yesterday.

Second purchase: motel room on Cable Beach Road. Neon hums, price charged by optimism.

Rekha elevates ankle, icing it with stolen minibar peas.

I call the burner line-silent test, then power it down. No trail, just pulse.

News scroll on borrowed Wi-Fi:

`Fair Work confirms human-trafficking angle, owner 'Dada' missing.`

Hamid's name spelled wrong; Trang still a "Vietnamese male, unverified."

I bookmark, heart rate deadpan.

Clock flips **11:48 p.m.**

Rekha sleeps in compressed breaths, or at least rehearses it.

I sit on the carpet, back against the minibar, ledger open in head:

Ute - forfeited

Fuel - zero

Freedom - running cost TBD

Final chore: crack the SIM, type a message I won't send-
Roy: Exit fee negotiable. Consider relocation.

Draft saved, unsent, pocketed with the burner.

· · ·

Lights out. Fan creaks.

Outside, the Indian Ocean whispers itineraries I can't yet afford.

Inside, orchard sap still coats my fingerprints, but the horizon's stain is fresh, and fresh is the best lie in circulation.

Sleep arrives on lay-by terms- payable at dawn, accruing by tide.

49 SANDBAR MOTEL LEDGER

Broome, Saturday, 7 April 2018

Broome sweated like it was hiding something. So did we.

The *Sandbar Motel* wasn't beach-chic- it was six turquoise shacks pretending they didn't used to house road workers or ghosts. Shack #3 came with a lopsided ceiling fan, two cockroaches on retainer, and walls thin enough to hear your conscience tap-dancing at 3 a.m.

Rekha dropped her duffel like it owed her rent. No words. Just that stare-the one where you're too tired to cry and too guilty to sleep.

I checked under the floorboards. Butter knife, loose plank. Esky still there.

. . .

Fertiliser sack: thirty-eight thousand and change. Ledger: ziplocked, but sweating. USB: still inside the Rexona can. I screwed the lid tight, like that would hold back the storm.

Rekha didn't sit. She paced. A limp now, not from blisters, but from that thing we left in Kununurra. Buried shallow, breathing still optional.

"They'll come," she said.

"Of course they'll come." I didn't say *because we didn't bury him deep enough.*

The ABC ticker on the motel TV crawled like a blood trail: **ORCHARD BOSS MISSING — LABOUR CAMP RAID CONTINUES.** No names. Yet. But we knew that face would show up. Dada didn't die quietly. Men like him never do.

"We can't go back," I said. "Not to Melbourne. Not to Thomastown. Roy's boys, Trang's boys, now the cops-everyone's licking our scent."

She nodded. Then added, quietly: "There's one place."

. . .

A pause. A different kind of pause.

"My sister's in Perth."

I turned.

"What?"

She didn't meet my eyes. Just fished a folded piece of paper from her pocket, creased like it had been thought about, and unthought, many times.

"She's my mother's other daughter."

"The mother who ran?"

"She didn't run alone."

That landed harder than the motel fan clinking above us.

"She left you. And started again?"

"She left *us*. But she didn't disappear. Just rebranded."

. . .

And you didn't tell me, I wanted to say. But how could I complain? I hadn't exactly sent her a postcard from the mango grave.

"She owes me nothing," Rekha said. "But she has a flat. A front door. Wi-Fi. And not Dev."

The burner phone buzzed once - an unknown number. We didn't answer. Burners were for listening to silence, not making noise.

I grabbed my pack. "When do we leave?"

"Tonight. Greyhound depot. I've got cash. She won't like it-but she won't call the cops either."

"Why not?"

Rekha's face hardened like the Kimberley floor.

"Because she knows who our mother was. And what men like Dev do to girls like us."

. . .

We didn't sleep. The esky stayed shut. The USB stayed zipped.

Outside, the motel hummed with the quiet of swamp coolers and sins sweating through walls. The night rolled on, hot and still and vengeful.

Perth wasn't safety. But it was distance.

And sometimes, distance is the only version of justice you get to afford.

Rekha,

As our coach hums through darkness on the day we
left Broome, every vibration reminds me: the heaviest
thing in the luggage hold isn't a suitcase - it's the
secret I wedged between us.

I kept silent to spare your memories:

no image of me outside that Grey Street door,

no footage of your uncle cornered by the same kind
of gaze he once turned on you,

no sweat-glossed face handing over fifty thousand
dollars to buy distance from your life.

I told myself ambush was justified if it bought your
safety.

The lie has been grinding its teeth in my throat ever
since.

That night, under the aisle lights' cold halo, I finally
understood:

love is not a witness-protection program.

You deserve the full accounting - interest, hidden
fees, morally suspect receipts.

When we step off in Perth, I'll hand you everything:

the footage, the payoff, the stamped receipt that says
LOAN PAID IN FULL back in Pampady.

If the price is whatever trust I have left, I'll pay.

Secrets double their weight the moment the engine
stops.

This confession is the only bag I want to carry when
the sun splits over Wellington Street

and the driver tells us to claim what's ours.

**And I know - even if you didn't know it yet -
this is the last journey we'll take together.**

- A.

50 SOFT LANDING, HARD BORDER

Broome, Sunday, 8 April 2018

Greyhound Coach #481 coughs its way out of Broome just after dark, as if the engine has an allergy to farewells.

The vinyl seats smell like last night's fried fish, and everyone aboard has the same plan: **pay by the kilometre, keep their stories to themselves.**

Two hours south we stop at Roebuck Roadhouse, flood-lit like a crime scene.

Rekha limps across the concrete-her ankle's still swollen from the orchard chaos-and the servo lights stamp our shadows flat.

.   .   .

This isn't escape. It's just motion disguised as relief.

Every kilometre buys us time, not absolution.

My phone pings:

Joseph:

ABC ticker says overseer D'Rosario missing. Police confirm Trang's ID. Keep your head low.

Rekha reads it.

Pockets the dread like spare change, and climbs back on.

The coach drones through the night. She dozes, and I rehearse my inventory of sins:

• Roy's exit fee - doubled.

• A USB of orchard ledgers iced under a motel floorboard.

• Trang - permanently clocked out behind a shed.

• Dada - composting under Kimberley moonlight.

The air-con hisses like a priest who's heard it all before.

Just before dawn the bus spits us into Perth's terminal - buzzing neon, weak coffee, a mural that promises "Opportunity Lives Here" while the bins overflow.

•   •   •

We don't speak right away. Too much weight in our backpacks.

Rekha rubs her ankle, checks her phone, frowns.

"It's her," she says.

Her stepsister. The one we never talk about.

They speak for ten minutes. All I hear is the thud of her thumb pressing the screen harder than needed.

When she hangs up, she turns to me.

"The police called her," Rekha says. "Said I'm listed as a witness. That they need to speak to me. Urgently."

Pause.

"They asked if I was in touch with... anyone connected to the incident."

She doesn't say Dev. She doesn't need to.

I look at the floor like it'll give me a script.

. . .

"They're meeting me today," she adds. "I'll stay with her a few days. Just until I understand what's happening."

I nod too quickly.

"Of course."

What I don't say is: *You're safer there. Away from me.*

We split outside the terminal.

Her sister's Corolla pulls up. Beige. Clean. The kind of car that doesn't get pulled over.

They hug tightly. Not warmly.

Rekha glances back once, then slides into the passenger seat.

Window half-down. No goodbye.

I drag my bag three blocks until I find a hostel with a vacancy light flickering like a faulty pulse.

Shared dorm. Twelve beds. A$ 37 a night. Breakfast not included. Security optional.

My bunkmate's already snoring. The wall socket sparks if I breathe near it.

. . .

I zip my backpack closed around my shoes. Tuck the USB into the toe of one. Sleep in jeans.

In the morning, I try for work.

The hostel noticeboard has three sheets: **cleaning, kitchenhand,** and **"Customer Service – No TFN? No problem."**

I circle the third.

My hands still smell like mango sap.

That night, I sit in the hostel stairwell and rewatch the city lights flickering across the glass doors.

Every reflection asks the same question: *What are you still doing here?*

51 A FOREIGNER ON THE PHONE

Next day, I'm in a strip-lit office above a car rental in Cannington.

Headset tight. Shirt still scented with Broome.

They hand me a script and a name badge that says "Jay."

My job: **sell SIM cards to migrants who still think Australia is a promise.**

Nepali uncles. Tamil aunties. First-year students who apologise before speaking.

"Just A$ 25 to connect. Port your number. Free voicemail."

. . .

They don't ask if I'm legal.

They just ask if I can pronounce "international recharge" with confidence.

I can.

The room buzzes like a prayer hall reciting someone else's miracle.

Rows of us in formation - elbows aligned, accents tuned to global polite.

The trainer's South African, third-gen Indian.

She opens with a line she's rehearsed before:

"Everyone here's from somewhere. Nobody's from here."

Polite laughter.

The kind that doesn't touch your ribs.

My first call: a man in Geraldton who tells me to "go back to Islamabad."

I mark it **Resolved** and move on.

. . .

By day three, I've learned how to fake warmth.

By day four, I know everyone else is faking something, too.

Kunal, next to me, claims he's from Brisbane -

but mutters "Chennai traffic" in his sleep.

Mei, across the aisle, speaks six languages,

but tells customers she's "just back-end."

We aren't workers.

We're **voices**.

Disembodied. Agreeable. Designed to be forgotten.

Indians are the new migrant class.

But no one says it that way.

We say: **"highly skilled."**

We say: **"good cultural fit."**

We say: **"Let me just transfer you."**

What we mean is:

. . .

We're fluent in the art of being tolerated.

I meet a Ugandan woman - once a schoolteacher -

now says "I understand your frustration" thirty-seven times a shift.

A Nepali guy tells me his brother vanished after an immigration interview.

Didn't say **deported** -

Just: *"He's not on the roster anymore."*

In the break room, nobody says their visa status.

Instead, we ask:

• "You working tonight too?"

• "You getting weekends?"

• "You ever think about Canada?"

One night, I overhear a man on the phone - maybe Sri Lankan, maybe Fijian:

"If I stop working, they'll send me back.

And I don't even know where *back* is anymore."

. . .

He hangs up.

Looks at me. Doesn't blink.

"You hiding too?"

I don't answer.

My cubicle faces a wall. No window.

But sometimes I imagine standing up and saying:

"I'm not Jay.

I'm Arjun.

I sent a USB to the police.

I ruined a man.

I broke a woman.

I disappeared on purpose."

But I don't say that.

I say:

"Thanks for holding. Let's get that sorted out for you today."

52 EVERYTHING I DIDN'T SAY

Elizabeth Quay - Perth, Thursday, 12 April 2018

12.20 p.m.

We meet near the river.

Neutral ground. Mid-afternoon.

Sun off the water like glass shards - too bright to think clearly.

She brings food - half a wrap and two lemonades in a plastic bag.

I bring nothing.

Not even honesty.

We sit on a bench with peeling paint.

The kind that remembers too many breakups.

She doesn't ask how I'm sleeping.

I don't ask how her sister is.

Instead, she hands me the wrap and says,

"They knew your name."

She says it lightly.

Like she's just noticed a new item on a grocery list.

"The police," she adds.

"They called me in. Said it was informal. But they had a file. With names."

She unwraps her lemonade like it's a confession.

"They asked about the orchard. About Dev. About who helped me. About who photographed everything."

Pause.

She sips. Swallows too hard.

·   ·   ·

"They had screenshots. Guest lists. Call records. A timeline."

I nod.

Not too fast.

She glances at me, then looks away.

"They asked if I knew who sent it in."

She looks back.

"I said no."

Another pause.

"They asked again, like they didn't believe me. One of them just stared - didn't blink. I kept talking, but he was already deciding I was lying."

I say nothing.

She crushes the plastic cup a little too tightly.

"I think they're watching me."

.   .   .

I try to stay still.

"My sister says it's just nerves. But I know what watched feels like.

The orchard. The motel. Dev's office.

You don't forget surveillance. Not once it touches your skin."

She sets her phone face down between us.

"They mentioned a visa. Subclass 852 - trafficking witness.

If I cooperate. If I give them something."

I finally find my voice.

"What did you say?"

"I said I'd think about it."

She looks at me again.

Her eyes aren't angry.

Just tired of guessing.

She leans back. Breathes like it hurts.

.   .   .

"They said it was an inside job. One of the pickers, probably. Whoever photographed Dada's operation uploaded it before the complaint even landed."

I nod.

Say nothing.

Again.

Inside my chest:

I did it before.

To her uncle.

For cash.

For leaving her alone.

And she deserves the truth.

But I can't say it.

Not yet.

Not when saying it means changing how she sees me, again.

She picks up the phone, but doesn't check it.

"They think I'm hiding something," she says.

"Maybe I am.

Maybe we both are."

The wind picks up.

"I'm not sure what I'm allowed to call safety anymore," she says.

Then she stands. Gathers the wrappers. Doesn't touch me.

"I'll let you know what I decide," she says.

And just like that, the bench is empty.

53 HOW WE LEAVE EACH OTHER

Hyde Park - Perth, Friday, 13 April 2018

12.15 p.m.

I asked her to meet me the next day at Hyde Park.

Midday. Too bright.

The kind of sun that makes even hard truth look like it's sweating.

She came in her café uniform. White apron, arms crossed, hair tied like she'd run out of time.

She brought two samosas in a paper bag.

I brought nothing.

.   .   .

We sat under a tree that cast more leaf-shadow than comfort.

I didn't ease in.

Didn't build context.

Didn't soften.

I just said:

"It was me."

She blinked. Said nothing.

"Dev. The footage. The envelope. The timestamp. The charger cam. His sudden depature from Melbourne. It was all me."

Her expression didn't change.

That scared me more than yelling.

"I didn't tell you," I continued.

"Because I thought protecting you meant doing things for you. Not with you."

. . .

I watched her breathe - slow, deliberate, as if counting the words I wasn't saying.

"I didn't think you needed to know what it cost me. Or what it cost you."

She finally spoke. Quiet. Too quiet.

"What else didn't you tell me?"

Silence. My shoulders dropped like I'd lost something, but it had never belonged to me.

"Did you think I'd break?" she asked.

I shook my head.

"No. I think I did."

She turned toward the water. Wind cut through her hair, but she didn't flinch.

No tears. No drama.

Just recalculation.

. . .

Then she said the thing I deserved:

"You don't get to decide how I carry pain."

And then the thing I didn't:

"But thank you. For trying."

We sat like that for a while.

Two people on the edge of something that had already ended.

She handed me one of the samosas. I didn't take it.

"What happens now?" I asked.

She smiled, small and worn.

"You leave."

I stood. I didn't hug her.

She didn't cry.

I said: **"I'm sorry."**

She nodded.

Said: **"So am I."**

Everything I didn't say became part of the goodbye.

That night I booked a one-way ticket North.

Back to Broome. Or maybe just away from here.

I didn't delete anything in Joseph's folder.

Ord Valley Orchard - that's what it was called.

I didn't rename the files.

Didn't scrub the metadata.

Didn't hide behind aliases or zip passwords.

I added new ones.

The videos from Grey Street.

The files about Dev.

The ones that tracked Roy's ponzi interest ladder - name by name, suburb by suburb.

I deleted nothing.

I left it all.

Visible.

Searchable.

Open.

Because someday, someone's going to look.

And I want them to find everything.

On the bus out, I typed a message to her:

You don't need me to save you. But I hope someone listens better than I did.

I didn't send it.

I watched the screen until it timed out.

Then I let it go.

54 RED PINDAN DUST

Broome, Saturday, 14 April 2018

1:52 p.m.

Greyhound door wheezes, exhales twenty bodies and one neon courier bag.

The heat hits like unpaid interest: red pindan dust, smoke, a wet slap of coastal salt.

No one is here to greet me; Roebuck Bay hums beyond the car park, out of sight but inside every pore.

I shoulder the duffel-thrift-shop tarp stitched into a promise, and step onto ground the colour of oxidised debt.

A chalkboard outside the kiosk reads ***ICE COFFEE A$ 6.60***.

Six-sixty tastes like melted plastic, but it scours the bus stench from my tongue and buys me ninety seconds of shade.

Phone service limps to one bar.

Roy's last "EXPECT RECEIPT" sits unread, a digital land mine.

I follow the only taxi, not for a ride (fare charts laugh at broke students) but to hitch the first ten kilometres on foot—heat turns tarmac into mirage; mirage turns A\$ 14,000 passage money into hallucination.

Willie Creek track begins where bitumen runs out of conviction.

Red earth rises with each step, coating shoelaces, then tongue, then lungs.

Thirty-one minutes of plodding and a tin roof appears, crooked, sun-faded, crouched like it expects another cyclone.

Minh waits beneath, folding fishing nets that smell of old oceans and older disappointments.

Vietnamese, sixty maybe, nicotine grin sharp enough to cut rope.

"You Ar-june?" he asks, syllables bending like bamboo.

I nod.

"Fifty dollar week. Cash. You cook own rice."

We shake. His palm is sandpaper steeped in grease and regret.

He points: one bunk, half wall, bucket shower, dog sleeping underneath (or maybe deceased- no tail wag yet).

"Work tomorrow. Charter boats. Clean prop, scrape barnacle. Pay every Friday."

"Tide?" I ask.

"High water five-oh-four. King tide soon-good for crabs, bad for lies."

I don't ask what he means; lies rot quick in this heat, truth even faster.

Inside the shack, the air tastes of rust and evaporated regrets.

I drop the duffel.

Count the remaining bankroll: **A\$ 837.**

Subtract iced coffee, taxi bribe, Minh's rent: **A\$ 781.**

A\$ 14,000 to leave Australia -

if I find the right boat,

if nobody asks the wrong questions,

if luck shows up this time without a receipt.

Cukai the half-alive dog lifts one eyelid, decides against introductions.

I sit on the lower bunk, notebook out:

Assets:

• SD-card cash A$ 781

• Chain-store faith ±0

Liabilities:

• Roy Joseph ⌛

• Visa breach ⌛ ⌛

Rust settles on the page, stippling the margins like dried blood.

Minh calls from outside, needs help dragging nets into the shade.

Work begins before dawn here; debt never sleeps, but it can sweat.

As I step back into the kiln-heat yard, the horizon flickers-mirage or prophecy? Hard to tell when everything shimmers.

.   .   .

Still, something in this dust feels medicinal, a rough salve on blistered ambition.

Hope doesn't bloom; it clings like red grit to whatever dares to land.

I breathe once, twice, until my lungs agree to the new climate.

Then I bend to the nets, counting knots, counting hours, counting how many tides until the next domino tips.

55 THE CALL HOME

Broome, Sunday, 15 April 2018

7:46 p.m.

The shack smells of prawn shells and warm wire.

Minh's out. Cukai breathes under the table, still refusing to die.

One bar of signal hobbles in through the mesh window - the kind that lets you place a call but not escape what follows.

I dial *Achan's* number.

Let it ring.

Once.

Twice.

Twelve seconds of breath.

. . .

He picks up.

His voice is low. Not sleepy - **watchful**.

"*Mone?*"

I try to sound routine. "All okay here."

He doesn't answer that.

Then, quietly:

"They came last week."

The fan overhead stops turning. Or maybe it just gets quiet enough to hear its guilt.

"Who?" I ask.

Already knowing.

"Two men. Said they were from Roy's office. Didn't show ID. Said it was... 'exit formalities.'"

Pause.

Background: shop shutter, maybe a pharmacy drawer sliding.

"What did they want?"

"They said the loan is still open. Exit fee not cleared. They asked about your passport. About your new number."

Silence.

"Did they threaten you?"

My voice breaks without volume.

He clears his throat. "No. Not directly."

Which is worse.

Malayalee for *yes, but I didn't flinch.*

"Amma?"

"She hasn't told anyone."

Then, more quietly:

"But she started keeping the shutters closed even during pharmacy hours. That's not like her."

. . .

A second pulse joins mine in my throat.

"I'll fix it," I say.

No answer.

He sighs- long, like he's pouring something down a drain.

"Arjun," he says.

Not *Mone.*

Not *Eda.*

Just my name.

"We didn't come this far for this."

I want to say *I know*, but it won't land.

I say: **"I'll call soon."**

He just says, "Stay dry."

And hangs up.

I lower the phone.

Watch the bars disappear like a spine caving in.

. . .

Trang's ghost is in every shadow now.

The newspaper leak, the orchard fallout, the whispers in Perth.

They'll be connecting names soon.

Maybe already have.

And when they do, my family's name is still stapled to mine.

———

Notebook. New page.

Title: **To Kerala.**

"Evidence of debt cycling. Names cross-linked between Laxmi Financials, Gulf-Retour Properties, and campus agents in three districts."

"Roy Joseph. Independent operator. No banking licence. Hires collectors from within church youth wings."

"Photos pending. Recordings available."

I seal it into an encrypted ProtonMail draft.

Subject line: **'Godman Credit: Tip-off, more to follow'**

Recipient: **Anil Kurian, Malayala Daily - Reporter, Crime Desk.**

I don't send it.

Not yet.

But I let it sit.

Visible.

Unsent.

Alive.

The press knows how to dig.

So does Roy.

Let's see who gets there first.

56 THE LIGHTER AND THE MATCHBOOK

11:32 a.m.

Minh's out checking crab traps.

I'm inside, cross-legged on the floor, fan coughing in the corner.

Outside, the tide is low and the police scanner is loud: Trang's name floating through the frequencies like a bloated body no one wants to claim.

My laptop wheezes awake.

The folder's still there:

/RoyJoseph_Ledger/

Inside: screenshots, voice memos, loan slips signed in six states, two countries, one church hall.

. . .

I click open **'Kerala Chain 2016–17.csv'** - names cross-pinned between a Gulf-returned shell company and five engineering colleges.

A video follows. Roy's voice: slick, breathy, the same tone he used with *Achan*.

"Exit fee is flexible - your mother can cover it if needed. We don't mind who bleeds, so long as someone pays."

I hit record on a message.

Straight to Proton.

To: *Anil Kurian*

**Malayala Daily, Crime Desk*

Subject: *Godman Credit: Tip-Off #1*

Hi Anil,

You don't know me, but you know the type.

Roy Joseph. Alias collector. Loan agent. Ponzi priest.

He runs exits like he's running a pilgrimage - promises blessing, delivers silence.

This folder includes:

– Loan slips

– Fake guarantor IDs

– Exit fee threats

– Internal call logs (partial)

More can follow, depending on what you do with this.

If this gets buried, the rest goes elsewhere.

You print, I keep the tap open.

- A witness with no temple left.

I attach six files. Encrypt. Hit send.

The moment it disappears, I know the real countdown has begun.

———

4:18 p.m.

Phone buzzes.

Unknown number.

I let it ring once. Twice.

Then swipe.

. . .

"Is this the person who sent the Roy files?"

Voice like burnt coffee.

Professional.

Hungry.

"Depends who's asking."

"Anil Kurian. Malayala Daily. We're running a soft story tomorrow. No names. Just the system. But this-this can go deeper. You sitting on more?"

"A mountain."

"You willing to give it slowly?"

"Only if someone listens fast."

He pauses.

Then:

"You're not the first person to send me Roy's name. But you're the first to send proof. Actual paper."

. . .

"And if Roy calls you?" I ask.

"He already did."

A beat.

"Didn't like being described as a spiritual gangster. Said he'd sue."

"Good. That means it's working."

I hang up.

Window reflects my face: salt-slick, eyelids war-ready.

Roy will move now.

Not to counter the article.

To cut the source.

Which is fine.

Let him come sniffing.

The second folder's already backed up in three clouds and one cold SD.

.   .   .

And if the police knock before Roy does,

at least this time,

I go down holding a lighter and a matchbook.

57 THE ULTIMATUM

6:09 p.m.

Roebuck Bay bleeds orange.

Minh's boat ticks quietly as it cools.

A crab shell floats by like a warning.

I've waited two days.

For Roy to show his teeth.

Instead, he's been pacing the shoreline of my inbox - silent, but circling.

But I know the signal.

One press leak, and the king gets off his throne.

. . .

I step outside, phone to my ear, thumb hovering over one number that never lost its threat.

ROY JOSEPH – +91...

Still saved. Still loaded.

I hit call.

Two rings.

Three.

He answers like he's been chewing glass.

"So."

That's it.

No hello.

No how's your father.

I speak first.

"You've read the article."

. . .

He breathes through his nose.

Thick. Controlled.

"Half-page bullshit. Anonymous source. CBI won't bother."

"They will."

I keep my voice low, clear.

"You're not the headline, Roy. You're the pattern. I gave them a pattern."

He chuckles.

No mirth.

"What do you want?"

"Close the loan."

"The principal's paid."

"So close it."

. . .

"And the exit fee?"

His voice softens, menacing.

"That's what comes after the confession. The interest you pay for leaving quietly."

I don't blink.

"I have your full ledger. If I go quiet, it goes loud."

He pauses.

Then:

"You think this is India? You think Broome is far? I know your father's shop schedule better than you do. I know your mother still forgets to lock the side door at 4:00."

Blood drains from my tongue.

"You say one more word about them-"

"No. You listen."

His voice now steel-wrapped.

"You made noise. Now you'll bleed for it. Send another file, and someone will visit your family. Maybe they won't speak. Maybe they'll just wait outside until closing time."

. . .

Silence.

I let it sit.

Then:

"Come to Broome."

"What?"

"I'll pay your ticket. Economy, of course. You want the rest of your 'exit fee'? Come take it in person. Let's end this chapter properly."

A beat.

"You're bluffing."

"Book the flight. I'll text the address. I have got a spare bunk and zero curiosity."

He doesn't reply.

Just breathes.

. . .

"Bring a receipt," I say.

"Let's settle the books."

I hang up.

No tremble.

I sit on the edge of the shack's step.
The crab shell bumps the wood, bobs, floats on.

It's not just about the money anymore.
It's about what fear did to *Achan*'s voice.
About *Amma's* shutters.

Let Roy come.

I'll serve him cold beer.
And when he threatens me -
really threatens me -
I'll close this story like I close a ledger.

Hard spine. No refund.

58 HOW TO KILL A LOAN

Broome, Saturday, 21 April 2018

5:42 p.m.

The ocean is glass.

Flat. Still. Watching.

Minh's boat rocks faintly against the pier like it's holding its breath.

I sit on an upturned bucket, watching the last flight from Perth smear contrails across the sky like exit wounds.

6:01 p.m.

Roy steps off the gravel like he's been here before.

White shirt, aviators, carry-on that probably isn't carrying much.

Looks the same: clean moustache, oily gait, half-buttoned confidence.

He walks with the slow entitlement of someone who's never had to run.

"So this is exile?" he says, gesturing at the shack, the salt, the red dust sticking to his shoes.

I shrug.

"Cheaper than therapy."

He doesn't smile.

Just pulls out a folded sheet - my original loan document, creased at the corners, smug with memory.

"You brought the money?"

I gesture to a tin lunchbox.

It's packed with A$ 20s - Minh's crabbing money and mine, pinched from corners, peeled from shame.

. . .

"Take it. And delete the file."

"Which file?" I ask.

He steps closer.

Too close.

"You think this wins? A few leaks to Malayala Daily? You're a child with a lighter near a petrol station. I've outlived bigger scandals."

I nod.

"And what about CBI?"

His face tightens.

Just for a second.

"You know what I hate about debtors?" he says.

"They forget who opened the door for them. You want to burn me? Fine. But your parents... they still live in the same town. And I know who rents the apartment above the pharmacy."

There it is.

The threat, naked.

No interest rate. No discount.

He leans in.

"You think I don't have people in Broome too?"

I don't blink.

I don't flinch.

I just say:

"Then I guess it's time we settle the account."

—————

6:07 p.m.

He's bent over the lunchbox, counting bills with one eye and smirking with the other.

I move before I know I've moved.

One hand around his throat.

The other pushes him backwards- into the boat.

He stumbles, gasps, but doesn't yell.

He's too proud.

.   .   .

We fall together - into ropes, crates, heat.

His elbow grazes my temple.

My knee finds his ribs.

He hisses, wheezes, still fighting, even now.

Until he says it:

"They'll never stop, you know. Even if I disappear, someone will come."

And then he makes the mistake.

Whispers:

"Your *achan* bleeds easy."

Something goes cold in me.

Then loud.

I grip tighter.

Thumb under jaw.

Weight forward.

Boat rocking.

.   .   .

No blade.

No gun.

Just breathe.

Then the absence of it.

———

6:18 p.m.

Minh is waiting on the jetty.

He says nothing.

He sees the body.

Sees the anchor chain.

The tarp.

The tide.

He lights a cigarette.

Hands me the other.

"You cook tomorrow," he says.

Then helps me tie the knots.

———

7:02 p.m.

We take the boat out.

Far enough for the sky to forget us.

No ceremony.

Just gravity.

Roy disappears like a weightless secret.

No splash.

Just silence.

Just sea.

———

7:20 p.m.

Back on the pier.

Lunchbox still there.

Untouched.

I delete nothing.

The files stay.

So does the message.

Roy Joseph:

Settled. In full.

But the ledger?

Still open.

Because the ones who open doors -
sometimes you have to lock them out yourself.
Sometimes you bury them offshore.

59 THE SEA

Broome, Sunday, 22 April 2018

The sun rises like a secret - slow, red, half-regret.

Roebuck Bay steams under it, quiet as a confession sealed in an envelope with no return address.

Minh's boat still rocks, faintly.

You wouldn't know it carried a body yesterday.

That the sea took something it might one day give back.

He fries rice without looking at me.

Doesn't mention the rope burn on my knuckles or the fact that I haven't spoken since we docked.

.   .   .

"Crab nets today?" he asks, as if yesterday was just another delivery.

I shake my head.

"Tide's high."

"So?"

"So you need to be still."

———

Down by the water, I sit cross-legged on red sand gone pale with morning.

Cukai limps past me, still alive. Somehow.

That dog and I, we're the only witnesses left.

The horizon is pure fiction - sky pretending not to remember.

I take out the notebook.

Cross out Roy's name.

One line. Black pen.

Under it, I write:

Trang: silence delivered.

Dada: buried in quotas.

Roy: returned to sender.

But this isn't closure.

This is salt.

The kind that keeps wounds open longer.

I didn't do it for justice.

Didn't even do it for *Achan*.

I did it because I needed someone to stop being a god in my story.

And when Roy wouldn't step down, I erased him.

Page one.

But even murder leaves margins.

And silence, once kept, starts writing its own footnotes.

I wade knee-deep into the surf.

Let the water take the last of Roy's voice from my skin.

He threatened my family -

but it's his echo that still rings in my ribs.

. . .

You think it's over, he said.

You think you're safe.

I bend.

Let the sea touch my face.

No prayers.

Just breathe.

Just brine.

Behind me, the shack waits.

Files still backed up.

One folder unopened.

The one with my name on it - and everything I haven't forgiven myself for.

Minh calls out from the porch.

I walk back.

Not healed.

.   .   .

But not hunted.

For now.

60 BURN NOTICE

The sea changes colour the moment you decide to leave.
Turns from rust to surrender. From memory to permission.

I watch it from a dune that smells like low tide and burnt oil,
thumb pressing the lighter in my palm.

Behind me: one motel room, scorched laminate table, plastic
bag of documents zipped into silence. Orchard ledger,
Trang's blood still digitally echoing inside.

Next to it: Roy's burner phone.

Still locked. Still full.

Still ticking.

.   .   .

I drop the pen drive into a tuna tin, drown it in methylated spirits, and set fire to my alibi.

Blue flame flickers. Sap and data hissing their last secrets. The tin glows like confession.

———

20:42 - Broome Jetty

Surya arrives late. Trawler boots, mullet, and a dog that won't stop growling at my duffel bag.

"You're not the first," he says. "Won't be the last. You bring cash?"

"Four grand. Half now, rest if I make land."

"Rote? You sure? Timorese got short memory but long knives."

"That makes two of us."

.   .   .

He nods. Lights a cigarette with a broken Bic. The kind of man who doesn't flinch at blood, just invoices it.

"We leave on the midnight tide. You breathe, you stay. You speak, the sea answers."

———

10:19 pm

I roll up everything left: burner SIMs, Rekha's hair clip, Roy's last invoice.

Toilet flushes half of it. The rest burns in the sink. Smells like cloves and guilt.

I leave the key under the mat. The front desk kid won't ask. He saw my eyes at check-in.

———

11:00 pm - Docks

Cukai, Surya's mutt, pisses on a rusted anchor. Surya hands me a tarp and says nothing.

. . .

I climb aboard Bayar Nanti. The deck creaks like it's already judged me.

Below: one mattress, one water bottle, two barrels of stolen time.

I breathe in burnt air and the absence of forgiveness.

Above me, the Broome sky folds into itself.
No stars. Just heat and consequences.

At exactly midnight, the engine coughs once.

Then again.

Then we move.

———

Somewhere behind me, Roy is already decomposing.

Somewhere ahead, a new name waits for my mouth to forget the old one.

FILE FIVE
കടവ് · KADAVU
CROSSING

Night boat crossing-Timor Sea to Beirut- iron psalms, forged names baptised in salt. Brown skin carried by wind, hush, and cities that don't ask questions: Rote, Kupang, Jakarta, Bali, Muscat. Beirut waiting like a quiet verdict.

61 BAYAR NANTI

Broome Mangroves, Wednesday, 25 April 2018

Broome tides don't whisper - they file statements.

The mangroves mutter names. Mine floats near the top.

Surya shows up two hours late, sunburnt and already chewing his own patience.

Fisherman by trade. Smuggler by necessity. Storyteller by accident.

His boat's name is **Bayar Nanti**.

Malay for *Pay Later*.

Paint peeling like someone tried to erase the promise.

· · ·

He snorts when I offer cash.

"Pay now, forget later. That's what people like you want."

He means brown skin with secrets. He means backpacks zipped over stories no longer legal.

I show him the passport: Indian, limp, water-stained, no longer laminated with hope.

"I need out."

"Out has many destinations," he says, scratching at a tattoo of a shark mid-vomit. "You want forgotten or just missing?"

I say, "I want the kind of missing that doesn't echo."

He spits sideways. "That's offshore rate. Four grand."

I hand over A$ 4,000 like it's hush money for my own reflection.

———

We meet again at high tide.

Moon fat. Wind slow. Roy's ghost already whispering into the mangroves like static trapped in a curtain.

"You sure you didn't leave anything behind?" Surya asks.

I left Roy.

Locked in a tin shed behind the servo, ankles tied with nylon netting, last voice note still ringing on my burner phone.

His last words?

"This country forgets debt. But not interest."

I had no answer. Just one rusty padlock and a shovel I never used.

———

Cukai, Surya's mutt, pisses on the hull and growls at me.

Instinct. He knows.

Boat smells like rot, betrayal, fish guts, and something older than confession.

I climb in anyway.

.   .   .

Below deck, there's room for me, one duffel bag, and a fever.

The pen drive jabs my thigh. It holds:

• Orchard rosters.

• Payslip forgeries.

• One grainy photo of Dada's knife reflecting moonlight just before it disappeared into Roy's ribs.

The first engine coughs like it's choking on evidence.

The second gurgles like it remembers a sin.

Surya hums a sailor's song in Bahasa, slow and off-key:

Kalau mati di laut, jangan pulang...

If you die at sea, don't come back.

I think of *Amma*, crouched in the back kitchen in Pampady, peeling shallots with her thumb still bandaged from the last pawn receipt she signed.

Of *Achan*, opening the shop at 9:05 a.m., because grief runs on Kerala Standard Time - five minutes behind, always apologising.

Of Rekha, who once said:

"You carry ghosts like luggage, Arjun. I only carry what I can burn."

She burned me.

Or maybe I burned first.

I didn't flee. I expired in a direction.

———

We pull away from the mangroves.

Broome shrinks behind a curtain of salt haze and unpaid debts.

Cukai barks once, sharp, accusatory.

I pretend it's a blessing.

Surya cuts the engine once we hit open swell.

Points to where the stars should be.

"Rote. Five nights, maybe six. If the wind doesn't get political."

I ask, "And if it does?"

.   .   .

He shrugs.

"Then you meet the kind of god who doesn't read passports."

I lie back, arms folded behind guilt.

Sky black. Water louder than thought.

My name is Arjun Ajith Nair.

I have A$ 14,000 left, no country, and a dog that keeps growling like it knows I forgot to bury something.

Maybe I did.

Maybe that's why the sea smells like pepper beef, turmeric sweat, and the night *Amma* caught me lying about the loan.

Somewhere below the boat, the past circles - patient, dorsal-finned.

I hold my breath.

The boat keeps going.

. . .

Because Bayar Nanti always floats -

until the invoice arrives.

*Rekha, imagine a fishing trawler named **Pay Later**-truth in advertising, really. Up here, the currency is barnacle scrapings and sputtering karma; I traded both for six square metres of deck that smells like dried squid and overdue invoices. Everything on board is an IOU: air I haven't earned yet, sleep deferred until the sea permits. The water lies flat, the way a crouched dog lies flat, calm only because it hasn't chosen its victim. I've taped the USB-orchard ledgers, Roy's exit-fee arithmetic, to the underside of the lifeboat seat. If this hull folds, evidence floats longer than any of us.*

I try to picture you in Hillarys, but distance pixelates your face into something low-resolution and heartbreak-proof. Each wave that slaps the bow feels like punishment; the one that follows feels like penance, and neither gets me closer to absolution. So I keep turning the same

*question in my head, the way a tongue
prods a cracked tooth:*

**If every kilometre of my freedom is
    bought on credit, do I still deserve a
    space in the memory of someone
    whose debts were never of her
    choosing-**
**or should I drift out of frame and let
    your ledger finally close without
    charging any more interest?**

*The engine drones on, the IOUs stack higher,
    and somewhere under the haze, a
    stopwatch with no face keeps counting what
    neither of us owes but both of us feel.*

62 SEA LIKE A STOMACH

Timor Sea, Thursday, 26 April 2018

Day One

Broome coughs us out like food poisoning.

The sea doesn't accept.

It digests.

Bayar Nanti rocks like a father who never learned to hug.

———

Cukai paces the deck, pisses on the cooler again.

Surya hums to the compass, not to me.

I stare at the horizon long enough it starts to retreat.

Salt clots my lips.

Guilt does the rest.

———

Night One

The sky opens with a zipper. No moon. Just cloud fungus.

I dream Roy is still alive.

He's not in the tin shed.

He's in the hull.

Laughing.

"You think the sea can drown debt?"

I wake up chewing on my own tongue.

Blood. Salt. The flavour of unfinished revenge.

———

Day Two

I vomit into a bucket that might once have held bait.

Or evidence.

Surya says nothing. He lights a smoke and mutters to Cukai.

He calls me *"the cargo with eyes."*

———

That night I remember Rekha's laugh -
how it sounded like a spoon against a steel plate.

We used to lie on the floral doona and talk about
what we'd name the dog we'd never afford.

She said: "You'll name it Debt, and still not train it."

———

Mid-voyage
The GPS blinks like a dying conscience.
One bar.
No signal.
Still, the guilt comes through.

———

I hallucinate:
• *Amma* reading the last pawn receipt by candlelight.
Her thumbprint still bleeding.
• *Achan* swallowing the phone bill.

"Melbourne call charges, *mon*. They bill by the minute. Like shame."

• Rekha licking mango sap off her wrist like she wanted to erase Dada's fingerprint.

———

The pen drive slides in my pocket.

Not quite evidence.

Not quite absolution.

I consider throwing it overboard.

But it might float.

Like all my worst ideas.

———

Day Four

Storm.

Not cyclone. Not mercy. Just wind having an argument with the past.

Cukai howls. Surya straps the cooler shut like it's a confession box.

I press my face to the deck and tell it everything.

It listens.

———

Sea like a stomach.

Sour. Gurgling. Unforgiving.

It doesn't purge you.

It makes you re-chew every mistake you ever swallowed without reading the label.

———

Night Five

Surya spits overboard and mutters: "Rote tomorrow. If the sea signs the paperwork."

I nod. My skin has blistered where sun met regret.

———

I close my eyes and write this chapter on the inside of my skull:

1. One passport, Indian. Water-damaged. Smells like curry leaf and second chances.

2. One pen drive. Orchard wages. Unpaid blood.

3. One girl who ran toward the cops.

One man who ran toward the sea.

———

Tomorrow I will buy a new name.

But tonight I am still **Arjun Ajith Nair**.

Still a boy from Pampady who packed pepper pickle and came home with salt scars.

Still afloat.

Barely.

Until the sea decides if I'm worth the paperwork.

63 ROTE, OR THE CLOSEST I CAME TO A GOD

Rote, Monday, 30 April 2018

Land appears like guilt-slow, green, and undeniable.

Surya stabs the throttle. Bayar Nanti lurches. Cukai growls like he knows we're crossing from fugitive to fraud.

Rote Island rises ahead, quiet as a Sunday hangover.

Palms lean sideways like gossiping uncles.

Somewhere in the haze: chickens, a burning tyre, maybe God.

———

We beach in a curve of grey sand between two fishing nets and three forgotten flip-flops.

No customs, no clocks. Just one boy watching with the detachment of a saint who's seen better sinners.

Surya tosses me a half-dry towel and grins.

"You want ceremony? Wrong island."

————

The boat spits me out.

Cukai barks twice, then pisses on my duffel bag for the final time.

Baptism, I guess.

————

We walk inland. No path. Just memory of one.

Heat presses down like a bureaucrat's rubber stamp.

A hut appears, held together by promises and eucalyptus. Inside: a plastic table, a Jesus calendar from 2017, and a man named **Benny**.

He doesn't look up. Just mutters, "Indian? Or Timorese who studied too hard?"

———

I hand him A\$ 3,000 in sweaty fifties. He sniffs the bundle like it might confess.

Then opens a drawer full of *second lives.*

Birth certificates that never saw a cradle.

Passports with names more stable than the men who carried them.

One fresh ID: *Jose Manuel da Costa*, born Ermera, Timor-Leste, Catholic, apolitical, blessedly forgettable.

———

Photo booth? No.

Benny lifts a cracked iPhone.

"Smile like your mother died."

———

Click.

Click.

Done.

———

New me arrives laminated and with more faith than the old one.

My reflection in the plastic looks halfway between penitent and postcard.

Benny says: "This one will pass. Just don't test it in Singapore. They read fonts."

————

That night I sleep in a hammock that smells like mildew and deferral.

I eat grilled cassava. I drink something coconut-adjacent.

I dream of *Amma* slicing raw mango with oil-slicked fingers.

Of *Achan* opening the pharmacy gate before sunrise to beat the debt collector's bike.

I dream of Rekha with her feet in the mango bucket, saying:

"Soft hands don't survive storm fruit, Arjun."

————

The sea laps the shore like it forgot it tried to kill me.

I don't pray.

But I whisper "thank you" to the sand.

To the hut.

To Benny.

To the burnt tyre.

To whatever strange god took one look at me and said: *"Fine. One more chance."*

————

Morning arrives like an invoice.

Surya is already loading Bayar Nanti with sacks of something that doesn't want a receipt. He doesn't wave goodbye.

Cukai just stares.

————

I put on a shirt two sizes too big.

Stuff the passport into the duffel.

Tape the pen drive to my thigh.

And walk toward Kupang like I was born there.

————

I am no longer Arjun Ajith Nair.

I am Jose Manuel da Costa.

. . .

Ermera-born.

Debt-free.

Faith unknown.

———

And that night, in the shadows of a coastal town that smells of oil and drying fish, I sleep like a man who has finally learned to breathe without being watched.

Just once.

64 THE GIRL WITH THE COUNTRY ON HER BACK

Kupang, Thursday, 3 May 2018

Kupang smells like expired prayers and clove cigarettes.

The kind of city where old ships creak in the harbour like they're trying to confess.

Where rats know which alley hides real money and which just smells like fish.

———

I arrive on the back of a chicken truck, duffel between my feet, *Jose Manuel da Costa* folded in my chest pocket like a birth certificate forged by mercy.

The border guard looks at the ID, then at me, then at his bowl of instant noodles.

Stamps the visa anyway.

Not because he believes it - because it's lunchtime.

————

A girl watches from the far end of the queue.

Short. Lean. Eyes like cracked marbles.

One side of her head buzzed short, the other hidden behind a curtain of cheap black dye.

On her neck, just visible above the collar of a hoodie two seasons out of style:

a map.

Tattooed in black ink. Rivers, lines, mountains - the whole of Myanmar.

And a word in Burmese script: မိခင် - *Mother*.

————

She sees me looking.

"You speak?" she asks, accent somewhere between Mandalay and mid-flight.

"No," I say. "But I can read the silence."

————

We share a bench outside the immigration shack.

She flicks sunflower seeds into the gutter.

Says her name is **Thiri**, but shrugs like it's borrowed.

"You Portuguese?" she asks, eyeing my fake ID.

"Timor-born. Catholic. Clean," I say, reading off the backstory Benny gave me like it's a menu I can't afford.

She smiles, small and sharp.

"Everyone here is lying. Some of us just do it better."

———

Over lukewarm soto ayam and sweet tea that tastes like regret melted in syrup, she tells me:

• She was smuggled through Maesot, Thailand, hidden in the luggage compartment with two other girls and a puppy.

• She worked six months in Penang, folding shirts that would be sold to people who call her country a headline.

• She got caught with someone else's SIM and traded a smile for mercy.

• Now she's heading for Bali - like everyone else who wants to disappear without paperwork.

———

At the guesthouse, she pays in crumpled rupiah. I pretend to be her cousin.

We share a fan.

We sleep top and tail.

She snores like a kitten with trauma.

————

That night, a brownout hits.

The fan dies. The room chokes on sweat and old dreams.

We lie still. Breathing.

She whispers, "Do you ever think about the people who loved you before you became this?"

I say nothing.

She says, "I do. Every night. Until I forget their names."

————

Before dawn, she draws the map again - this time in steam on the bathroom mirror.

. . .

"Where are you headed?" I ask.

"East," she says. "Or maybe just inward."

She offers me her extra charger. A bite of her bread.
And a warning:

"Bali lets you vanish. But it charges rent for silence."

———

At the terminal, she boards a boat bound for Larantuka.

Disappears into a bus full of Australians pretending to be
adventurers.

I stand there with a duffel bag full of lies and a head full of
ghosts.

Rekha's voice returns for one line:

"If you want to vanish, you have to stop needing to be found."

———

I buy a SIM.

Book a flight to Jakarta.

Eat the last sunflower seed she left on the windowsill.

Tastes like husk and almost-forgiveness.

65 JAKARTA: CITY OF PROXY LIVES

Jakarta, Monday, 7 May 2018

Garuda Flight 462 lifts off like it's tired of being a country.

I sleep through take-off, wake just before landing.

In between: dreams of Rekha whispering my name
backwards.

Arjun becomes *Nurja* - not quite reborn, just harder to trace.

———

Jakarta is a furnace pretending to be a city.

Everything here sweats: buildings, traffic, intentions.

I step onto tarmac that smells like petrol and paper cuts.

. . .

My name is **Jose Manuel da Costa**.

My birthday is now in August.

My country of origin is plausible but inconvenient to verify.

I keep repeating it under my breath like a rosary for liars.

———

Thiri was right.

Jakarta is a factory of **proxy lives**.

Every SIM card has someone else's face.

Every hotel guest signs under a name borrowed from a dead uncle.

Every Gojek driver has three phones and four backstories.

Nobody here is real.

Which makes it the perfect place to hide.

I rent a bed in Glodok, three floors above a shop that sells counterfeit iPhones and chicken porridge.

Wi-Fi cuts out when it rains.

Toilets flush like they're ashamed.

The manager is blind in one eye but can spot a fake passport at fifty paces.

"You quiet, pay on time," he says. "No trouble, no ghosts."

I nod.

Too late on both counts.

———

Work comes in whispers.

A man named **Koko** hires me to run deliveries for a ghost kitchen.

Not food - calories.

Rice, soy, regret.

We operate under ten apps, five aliases.

All registered to dead people with high reviews.

My shifts start at sunset.

I ride a busted Honda with stolen plates and prayers for brakes.

———

Every delivery I make, I wait for someone to say it:

"You're Arjun, aren't you?"
"From the mango farm?"
"The one who left Roy to rot?"

But the only names they call me are:

"Hey, abang."

"Bro."

"Driver."

"Wait."

Each one slices less.

———

In my spare time, I stalk the AFP website.

Nothing.

Roy's name hasn't surfaced.
No orchard reports. No missing man bulletin.

Maybe Broome has better things to remember.

Maybe mangroves forgive more easily than humans.

———

Still, I dream in fragments:

• *Amma's* bangles melting into pawn-shop receipts.

• *Achan*'s face when I lied about the scholarship.

• Rekha's silence on the last night before she ghosted me in Thomastown.

And sometimes - Roy.

Wearing his safari suit, standing knee-deep in mango sap, saying:

"You thought killing me cleared the ledger?"
"Debt always reincarnates."

———

One night, a Gojek rider recognizes me.

Not from Australia. Not from Roy's orbit.

· · ·

From Kerala.

2015.

A youth league debate.

He stares. Then blinks. Then smiles like we're still boys arguing minimum wage at a Rotary hall.

"You changed, macha. What happened to the MBA?"

I say:

"Switched degrees. Specialising in invisibility."

He laughs. Slaps my shoulder. Rides off.

But I don't sleep for two days.

———

I save up enough to buy silence.

Rent prepaid for three months.

A burner phone set to factory reset every 48 hours.

And an exit plan.

———

Bali.

Island of tourists, tattoos, and people who stopped asking questions.

It's time.

———

I send Benny in Rote a message from a borrowed SIM:

"Your Timorese nephew wants a beach job."

He replies with a 🐙 and a location pin.

———

I pack.

One change of clothes.

One passport in a false-bottom pouch.

One pen drive, still uncracked.

And a handful of Thiri's sunflower seeds.

. . .

Chewed down to shell, but they still taste like warning.

———

As I board the ferry out of Jakarta, I look back once.

The city doesn't care.

It forgets me faster than I forgot who I used to be.

And maybe that's the best mercy I've earned.

*There are moments when the universe shrinks
    to the glare of a ring-light and the hiss of
    melting laminate, and you realise
    identity is as negotiable as a bus fare.
In that Jakarta booth the photographer
    required only a smile-***"Smile, but not
    too honest,"*** as though honesty were a
    luxury item I no longer carried. So I flexed
    the approved muscles and let the
    laminator decide who I'd be next.*

*Walking back through Jalan Jaksa's damp
    neon, I slipped the fresh ID into my pocket
    and felt two pulses there-one plastic, one
    flesh-both claiming to be me. A self, I see
    now, is less a solid core than a stack of
    annotated drafts: the name Amma
    murmurs, the passport a government
    prints, the alias a smuggler sells, the silence
    that follows each trade. None erases the
    previous version; they simply crowd
    together, begging to be believed.*

The trouble with stacking selves is gravity.

*Each extra layer presses on the original
until the mirror shows an unfamiliar
composite and the old name feels like
someone else's ringtone. Reinvention
sounds heroic-burn the skin, walk away
lighter-but nobody mentions the ash that
clings to your lungs afterwards.*

*Boarding the night ferry to Bali, seawater
breathing brine and doubt, I grasped the
terms of the bargain: security in place of
authenticity, motion instead of belonging.
I sailed anyway-forward was the only
direction that didn't echo with footsteps
already taken-but halfway across the
strait, with nothing but dark water
beneath, a thought surfaced:*

**Rekha, if you met the man printed on
that new plastic,
would you even recognise the echo of the
one who left Pampady with you?
And if you wouldn't-do I still have the
right to chase your memory,
or does that belong to an earlier draft of
me you never agreed to revise?**

*The ferry kept its course, indifferent.
I stood at the railing, counting waves, unsure
whether I was running toward forgiveness
or away from identification.*

66 DENPASAR DELAY

Denpasar, Wednesday, 6 June 2018

Denpasar breathes in white tourists and exhales brown labour.

The airport smells like sunscreen, duty-free Calvin Klein, and immigration ink that never dries.

I land with a name that passes for Catholic, a duffel that doesn't smell like mango sap anymore, and a passport still damp from Rote sweat.

Jose Manuel da Costa.

Ermera-born.

Faith pending.

———

The immigration officer blinks at my page, twice.

"Timor?"

"Yah, sir. Family moved east. Never left." Smile tight. Voice gravelled.

Stamp.

Gate opens.

Blessed are the bureaucrats who don't overachieve.

———

Outside:

Taxis like vultures.

Surfboard messiahs in singlets.

Bintang logos tattooed on calves with ambition.

A woman selling SIM cards asks if I'd like *local or expat data.*

I don't ask the difference.

———

Kuta swallows me fast.

I get a bed in a hostel called **Sleeping Dogs**, shared with three Australians who whisper "Centrelink" like it's a prayer.

I work the till at a café that sells "raw brownies" for tourists and "real sambal" for the staff.

The owner is a French-Indonesian divorcee with two ex-husbands and one espresso machine she trusts.

She calls me **Manu** and doesn't ask for paperwork.

———

I count tips like a man rehearsing for rent.

At night, I wipe the machines down until they stop steaming.

Then I clean my conscience-unsuccessfully-with leftover espresso.

Rekha used to say I made coffee like I was grinding regret.

I still do.

———

Twist comes on day four.

. . .

It's always day four in these stories.

———

A guest checks in wearing a cap that says **W.A. Surf Patrol** and a gold chain that looks familiar.

He orders a long black. Stares too long at my name tag.

"Manu?" he says, testing the vowels like old currency.

"Yeah?"

"Looks like a cousin I used to know. Arjun or something."

Smile casual. Hands calm. Voice neutral.

"Don't know the guy. Sounds brown."

He grins. But the grin's lazy, like a trap not set for me but happy to reset.

———

That night I check the guest ledger.

· · ·

No surname. Just "Devon G."

I don't sleep.

———

In the morning, he's gone.

Bed stripped.

No checkout.

Just a business card left under the plate:

D. G. Solutions – Visa Advice & Study Abroad Support

Melbourne / Jakarta / Anywhere Else

On the back, in blue biro:

"Saw your hands shaking. You should fix that before someone official notices."

———

I pack.

No goodbye to the espresso machine. No tip box donation.

. . .

I take the first shuttle to the port, board a slow boat to Java with three Aussies, two monks, and a rooster in a laundry basket.

No ticket.

Cash only.

That's the currency of second lives.

———

As the island shrinks behind me, I whisper to the wake:

"Rekha-if I make it out, I'll name the dog after you. Quiet, suspicious, and smarter than I deserve."

The rooster crows like it caught the sarcasm.

———

South Lebanon calls. Or somewhere quieter.

But Bali taught me something:

Even paradise gets bored.
Even ghosts need visas.
Even Dev wears sunscreen.

67 THE SEA FORGETS IN ARABIC

Oman welcomes no one.

It simply nods and lets you pass through like heat through linen.

I arrive in **Salalah** on a cargo plane, manifest as a refrigeration technician.

The bribe was small. The silence after was larger.

———

The airport whispers.

Bags thump without echo.

Even customs look like they've been fasting for something bigger than Ramadan.

. . .

My passport - *Jose Manuel da Costa* - slides through untroubled.

Outside: heat thick as sandalwood paste.

Air sweet with frankincense, wet clay, and maybe divinity.

———

I take a room above a shop that sells prayer rugs and faded SIM cards.

The owner says nothing except "140 a week. No guests. No noise."

I nod.

Noise is expensive.

———

I walk the port at night.

Old dhows creak like they're trying to remember a route they haven't sailed in decades.

Boys sell mango juice in bags.

I drink two.

Throw up one.

————

On day two I get a job washing boats.

They hand me a bucket, a rag, and no instructions.

The work is honest.

Which means it hurts more.

Salt eats skin slowly.

My hands forget how to lie.

————

A man on the fifth boat stares too long.

Older. Skin the colour of teak.

Eyes sunburnt into slits.

He asks, in Malayalam-stained Arabic:

"You from Kozhikode? Or just another face from the monsoon?"

. . .

I say nothing.

He nods.

"I had a brother like you. Went missing into a dream. Still waiting for him to call."

He hands me a date from his lunch tin.

I eat it.

It tastes like sugar and old guilt.

———

The mosque down the road allows me to sleep under its fan if I pretend to pray.

I kneel twice a night.

Once for forgiveness.

Once for instruction.

So far, the silence answers both.

———

One evening, I hear a man reciting Qur'an near the harbour.

The verse curls through the air like a promise unclaimed.

· · ·

He pauses, wipes his brow, then says:

"The sea forgets in Arabic.
But only if you don't keep reminding it."

———

I stop speaking my name.
Even in thought.

Arjun Ajith Nair becomes breath.
Then background noise.
Then hush.

———

I stay eight days.
Long enough for callouses to form.
Short enough not to be remembered.

When I leave, the boat captain doesn't ask for ID.

Just says:

"Sit under the tarp.

If they ask, you're with the motor."

———

We sail north.

No paperwork.

No questions.

Just the engine and the sea - both louder than regret.

———

Next stop: **Beirut.**

Or something like it.

A city that doesn't care who you used to be,

as long as you pay in the right currency:

silence.

68 BEIRUT IS A VERB

Beirut, Thursday, 13 September 2018

We dock at dawn.

No horn. No flag. Just the kind of light that forgives nothing.

A port that smells like burnt wires, cardamom, and buildings that have collapsed more than once.

———

The man who smuggles me in says nothing during the crossing.

When we arrive, he points to the concrete steps and mutters:

. . .

"Don't look back. Beirut hates nostalgia."

———

I walk into the city wearing a cap that doesn't fit, a passport that doesn't belong, and the last usable lie in my pocket.

The buildings still wear their war wounds.

Some patched. Some proud.

Glass replaced. Memory never.

———

I get a room in a hostel that caters to NGO interns, burnt-out freelancers, and people whose passports smell of smoke.

My roommate is from Tripoli. His name changes every three days.

We bond over the shared language of erasure.

———

I find work washing glasses in a falafel shop in **Hamra**.

The owner hires me because I don't ask for lunch breaks and my Arabic is bad enough to sound harmless.

The kitchen radio only plays Fairuz.

Her voice slips between oil and tahini, reminding us that loss can sound beautiful if you sing it slowly enough.

———

At night, I drink tea on the roof with Sudanese workers and one silent man from Aleppo.

None of us talk about where we came from.

Only where we pretend to sleep.

———

One afternoon a man hands me his phone at the register and says:

"Talk to my cousin. He speaks English."

The voice on the other end says:

"You used to be Arjun, right?"

Click.

I walk out the back, throw the apron on a crate, and don't return.

———

Next day, I move to **Tyre**, south coast.

Quieter.

Fewer questions.

The sea looks tired here like it's trying to un-remember every boat it ever carried.

I rent a room above a tyre shop.

The landlord calls me "Mr. Da Costa" and assumes I'm from Goa.

I nod.

Let the lie stretch across the Mediterranean and wrap around my ankles.

———

Every week, I send US$ 100 to a post office box in Kerala.

Unclaimed.

Every week, I send it anyway.

Roy is dead.

Rekha is a ghost.

My father probably thinks I'm both.

But *Amma*?

She might still check the balance and wonder.

————

Beirut teaches you how to live among ruins.

Not beside them.

Within them.

It's a city where the glass glints, but never shines.

Where silence isn't peace - it's a negotiated ceasefire.

A city that doesn't ask for a name.

Only a reason to stay.

————

Mine is simple:

Here, the ledger doesn't follow.

Here, the mango sap can't stain.

Here, nobody picks fruit for someone else's quota.

———

I change my number.

I change my shift.

I change the way I walk.

But I don't change the dream:

Rekha walking barefoot into a coffee stall and asking,

"You still serve that burnt brew?"

And me saying,

"First cup's on the house.

The rest, we pay for together."

———

Until then, I wipe the counters clean.

And learn how to say *stay hidden* in Arabic -

softly,

like a verb that once meant love

and now just means

remain.

From: **Miguel Da Costa** <draft-autosave@protonmail.com>

To: **Rekha Gurung**

Subject: Draft #12 - when the trees stopped asking

Draft saved - 17 Nov · 06 : 22 a.m. - Tyre, South Lebanon

Attachments (1): kerala-stall.jpg

Rekha,

Olive season is gentle on aliases; the trees accept whatever name you prune under.

Here I'm just "Miguel," a man who clips branches at dawn, sips thick coffee at dusk,

and sleeps in a room without mirrors.

Most days I don't speak.

On the better ones, I hum.

This morning the postman handed me an envelope marked

To be held until claimed.

No stamp, no return address-only a blotted blue tear where a post-mark should live.

I almost tossed it, but the handwriting-small, crooked, unmistakable-stopped my hand.

Inside: one photo (attached).

A market stall in Kerala-coir mats, baskets, two jars of garlic pickle catching the sun.

Behind the counter:

- *Amma* in a washed-out yellow sari
- *Achan* with a pharmacy pen clipped to his pocket

Neither smiles; both simply wait.

On the back, in Malayalam, five words:

"Come when the interest ends."

No signature. No date. Just that.

I stared at it for an hour, then slid it into the notebook's back pocket-next to ferry

stubs, a passport I've out-lived, and the unsent voice note I once recorded for you.

The sea breeze shifted; Cukai (the dog who adopted me two villages ago) growled at nothing in particular, then curled back to sleep.

I tried your name aloud.

It didn't hurt-first time.

A moment later, beyond the orchard wall, a boy's voice-half-curious, half-certain-

called into the branches:

"Arjun?"

I haven't answered. Not yet.

When interest finally stops accruing-on loans, on lies-I might claim that name again.

Until then, I'm pruning silence into shape and counting down the seasons.

- still yours in the margins,

Miguel (for now)

Arjun (when the ledger clears)

ACKNOWLEDGMENTS

This book was written from the edges of systems, of countries, of belonging.

Like the protagonist, I too have sat across bank managers holding stamped rejections, and smiled through immigration counters carrying more debt than luggage. I've watched families remortgage futures so a name could be printed on foreign paper. And I've lived through the long, invisible work of learning to pass in accent, posture, ambition.

To everyone who's taken that same route: **I see you**.

This story owes a quiet debt to countless unnamed people who bent themselves to fit into new borders, new skins, and new alphabets. Thank you to the dreamers, the side-hustlers, the kitchen-shifters, the late-night letter writers. You are the archive this novel whispers to.

To my family, thank you for the sacrifices I didn't understand then, and still struggle to express now.

And to those reading this with a knot in their throat because parts of it felt too close: I hope you carry your name with less fear than the protagonist did.

And if not yet, soon.

ABOUT THE AUTHOR

Bobby Mohan is a Sydney-based writer born in Kottayam, India. After early schooling in Bahrain, he completed his higher education in India and Perth, Australia. He began his career as a journalist and advertising copywriter before pivoting into digital transformation, working with companies like IBM, Unilever, and Coca-Cola.

Having lived across Bahrain, India, Singapore, and now Australia, Bobby's life has been shaped by migration, identity, and reinvention- threads that run through his debut novel, *Brown Skin, White Lies*. He lives in Sydney with his wife, their dog Milo, and a WhatsApp thread that keeps him close to his son in Spain.

WORDS THAT CROSSED OCEANS

Malayalam, Malay, and other echoes from elsewhere

🏳 Malayalam / Indian English / Regional Terms
- **Amma** – Mother
- **Achan** – Father
- **Mon** – Son or boy (affectionate term)
- **Chechi** – Elder sister or respectful term for an older woman
- **Chettan** – Elder brother or respectful term for an older man
- **Etta** – Affectionate/informal version of *chettan*; often used by younger siblings or close friends
- **Mundu** – Traditional Kerala men's garment, like a sarong
- **Kadam (കടം)** – Debt
- **Kadavu (കടവ്)** – River crossing or ferry point
- **Veedu (വീട്)** – Home or house
- **COE** – Confirmation of Enrolment (student visa document)
- **Chenda** – Traditional temple drum
- **Ganapati** – Hindu deity, Lord Ganesha
- **Idli** – Steamed rice cake
- **Sambar** – Lentil and vegetable stew
- **Appam** – Fermented rice pancake
- **Chemmeen Fry** – Prawn fry
- **Pachadi** – Yogurt-based side dish
- **Guruvayoor** – Kerala temple town
- **Thiruvathira** – Kerala festival associated with women and dance
- **Matta rice** – Kerala's red rice
- **Palada payasam** – Sweet milk-rice dessert
- **Murukku** – Crunchy rice flour snack
- **Chilli powder / garlic pickle** – Common homemade condiments
- **KSEB** – Kerala State Electricity Board
- **Pampady** – Town in Kerala